Foreword

Authors Note & Important Information / Trigger Warnings

This book ends on a cliffhanger. The contents are occasionally very dark with triggering situations and scenarios, such as one explicit sexual assault scene, graphic violence, and explicit sexual situations. Please take these trigger warnings seriously. Your mental health is of the utmost importance.

Recommended for readers 18 years and older.

If you ever need to contact me, please feel free to do so at j.rdust_author@yahoo.com

Signed For You

J.R DUST

One

I need to find out what is going on. He is acting so sketchy and secretive – even more so than usual, but I can't ask Crow about it at home. There will be no chance of him telling me anything if Dad is around.

The rain is a relief. I am a winter lover - rainfall and all. I have only just walked out of my house, and yet I am thoroughly drenched. My favourite hoodie has droplets of rain being thrown its way. Even as a child I loved the rain. Dancing in the rain, making mud pies, and going on hikes, much to my dad's displeasure. Gray always used to play with me when Dad wouldn't, even though his friends always told him what a loser he was for hanging out with his little sister instead of them. It is one of the countless things I love about him.

I place my earphones in their rightful place, squeezing and moving them slightly to get them to fit just right. Looking down at my phone, I wipe away the droplets of rain that have already started appearing on its surface, click on the Spotify app, and put my running playlist on.

I look ahead at the houses beside my own, knowing that everyone that lives inside of them are no longer there apart from a few of the Cobras' wives. Not as though many of the men have wives around. Those that do are probably cooking their men dinner or cleaning the house in a hurry, running around after their children, or worrying about if their partners will come back tonight or not. It is never simple, never a certainty, always a worry. My father always promises me that he will return, and he hasn't disappointed me yet, even if he has returned home beaten black and blue on occasion. My dad is passionate about very few things, but keeping a promise is one of them. The others being me and the Cobras.

The Dark Cobras. His little, or not so little, part in the circle of men that surround us. He's in charge of them and the Clubhouse that so many of them call home. His best friend is the owner, the true Pres, so while he's in prison my dad is in charge. He nearly beat someone, or possibly multiple someones, to death. I was so young when it happened, no one ever really told me why he was gone, but I do remember hearing snippets of conversations. He asked my dad to take over his role, which as his best friend my dad gladly did.

I turn on my heel to look behind me as I hear Crow pounding down the steps after me. He's new to the Cobras, and he's been tasked with keeping watch on me – acting as my bodyguard.

My dad worries about me and thinks it will be best to have someone around, which I initially hated the idea of. I know it comes from a good place though, and sadly it often comes with good reason. I know that the dangers often lurk nearer than we would like, especially as a family member to a Dark Cobra.

My dad did his best by me though. He taught me to fight young, how to wield a knife and aim a gun. Now, just because he taught me, that does not mean that I am any good. I have admittedly never put my skills, or potentially lack of skills to the test, but I like to think that if I freeze and forget everything else, I could just kick whoever in the crown jewels and run. In my head that would totally work. I'm hoping I don't have to put it to the test anytime soon though.

"You couldn't have waited for me, Char? I've just searched the whole damn house for you!" Crow pants.

He's at the bottom of the steps that lead to our three-bedroom house, leant over catching his breath. He looks as if he's just run a marathon, not run around a small town house.

My eyebrows raise as I smirk at Crow. He's young, though he doesn't particularly look it. He's four years older than me. Just. He had his twenty-second birthday a few weeks ago, and he just loves to remind me how mature that makes him and childish it makes me. Even though I know he's only joking, it still drives me crazy.

He's been on my watch for about six months, and we've gotten to the point where we're inseparable, not just because he's there to guard me but because we get on a lot better than I think either of us expected.

He's still leant over catching his breath.

Good thing I hadn't turned my music up too loud or I wouldn't have had the luxury of hearing him huffing and puffing. I roll my eyes and start a slow jog away from my house, past the front of the other homes that belong to my dad's fellow men. I'm not sure how it started, if it was done on purpose or not, but so many of my dad's friends that work with him live on the same street as us, or in the Clubhouse full-time.

"We're running, Crow, get your arse into gear or you won't catch me at all." I turn around, jogging backwards, silently hoping that I don't trip over anything or anyone, keeping my pace as I yell at a still hunched over and out of breath Crow.

He brings his eyebrows together and looks at me with the same fiery look they all have when they're angry, and I can't help but smile.

Crow is about six foot in height, possibly even a little taller, so he overpowers my five-six appearance. He has shaved, short, jet black hair. Where my appearance is plain, with freckles covering my face and a healthy body to match, with no bones on show but not enough fat to actually call me chubby, he is

5

anything but plain. He has the most annoyingly perfect body, so much so that you can see through however many layers of clothes the man is wearing that his body is ripped. He has muscle everywhere and looks like he should be in some fighting ring, instead of following an eighteen-year-old girl around town.

We're opposites, Crow and I. He likes to act grumpy around practically everyone and yet I am happy. Well, most of the time. Most women, hell not even just women, most people in general would cower at the look of annoyance, anger, or frustration that the men around me seem to collect when they become part of Club life. It's got to be some sort of initiation. If you can't pull some crazy deadly face, then you can't join. I mean probably not, although that would be a funny rule to implement.

"Fuckin' hell, I hate you sometimes, woman." Crow sighs as he begins a light jog behind me.

I turn back around and face the road ahead once again as I speed up and turn the volume of the music that I'm listening to up so that it drowns everything else out, and then I run.

The rain is slowly stopping. It is now a slow intermediate shower of soft liquid falling from the grey clouds above.

Between the rain and the droplets of sweat running down my brow from the run, I don't notice that I'm at the place I need to be until I practically run into the large oak tree in front of me.

I transform my high-speed run into a gentle jog as I aim for the top of the hill above the park. The park is silent, not a person in sight. It's always overcrowded and filled with people throughout the summer, but at the peak of winter, around mid-January, there's no one around and there probably won't be anyone around for a few months to come yet. The hill I'm running up is one of the most popular hiking spots in Yorkshire, surrounded by forestry, biking paths, and little benches that are now rusty and breaking, desperately in need of some serious maintenance that it appears they haven't seen any of in years.

The trees protect me from the last of the rain. I sprint to the top of the hill, seeing my spot isn't far away. In the winter, no one bothers with this place, so until the summer arrives, with it being just four miles from my home, it's my favourite place to use for the peace I crave away from anyone else.

I grab my phone out of the pocket of my grey hoodie, panting from the run as I turn the music off and take the earphones out, folding the lead around my phone until it's neat enough to put back in its previous home.

Just as I reach the top and find the space between the trees where Crow and I made our makeshift shelter a few weeks ago to take a seat that allows me to see the park below, I turn back on myself, looking for Crow, and notice that he's still a little way behind me.

I sit down on the leaves, bark, and dirt on the floor, crossing my legs and take out my book, and my flask of tea as well as two cups from the backpack that I carried up here, pouring the still scalding water carefully into the camping cups and then placing one in front of me and one next to me, ready for Crow.

Reading is one of my greatest pleasures. I get through a different book every day or two. I love to read anyway, but I'll be starting university next year to study Publishing and English Literature, so part of my love for books comes from my desire to be a publisher. I tend to read and worship romance novels, albeit dark romance novels, but romance all the same.

I see love every day in my dad's fiery eyes, and that of the men and women around me, but it's not the kind of love that I yearn for.

Crow finally reaches the top and collapses beside me, picking up the camping cup filled with tea ready for him.

We sit in comfortable silence for a while, with me reading my book and Crow sat peacefully, between checking his phone and simply using the silence to breathe for more than a minute, between the Club's angst and drama.

The Clubhouse and The Dark Cobras seem to have this stigma attached to it. The stigma that allows everyone to think those inside of it are violent, angry, aggressive killers. They are the rumours and taunts I grew up with as a child, and although that's not completely inaccurate in some aspects, it's also a big fabrication in other areas. My dad does his best to keep me sheltered from the life he leads, though when he shows up wounded, there's only so much he can hide. I've read stories about motorcycle clubs, gangsters, the mafia, and so much more, and I'm sure that's what the little town around me perceives the Club and the Cobras to be, but it's not. It doesn't hurt to have them think that though, because it means people won't mess with you which is what my dad always reminds me. Let people think what they want as long as you know the truth.

"Did you put any sugar in the tea, Char? You know I need sugar in my tea." Crow and his obsession with having half a pot of damn sugar in his tea is madness. Six spoonfuls is his minimum – yes, minimum.

"There is sugar, Crow, just not enough to give you a heart attack and shut you up, sadly." I don't look at him as I speak, my attention still on the book in one of my shivering hands.

I turn back to my book, until I notice Crow moving in my peripheral. He's pushing himself up from the floor with one hand whilst still smoking with the other. As I look up at him, he takes off his leather jacket, embroidered with the Cobras emblem on the back, and puts it over my shoulders.

Immediately, I feel the weight of it. It's real leather and to be big enough to fit the giant next to me, it's bound to be too big for me which only adds to the weight around me, but I love it. I don't particularly like my body being on show. It's not as though I don't like it, although there are parts I'd change, the same as anyone I suppose, it's just for comfort that I love to wear things that overwhelm my body. That and my belief that I shouldn't need to show my body to receive the looks from men that my dad and Crow are certain I get constantly – I don't ever notice it but I don't argue with them either. I glance up at Crow as he reaches his hand out for me to take it. I do. His hands feel rough on mine, and for the millionth time since he came around, I wonder if there could ever be more. I've been feeling closer to him for some time, idly wondering if the possibility of more than what we have could ever be real.

"It's getting dark, let's take a stroll home before your dad gets back." His voice sounds rough, though not anywhere near as affected by the cold as what I'm sure mine would be if I said anything right now. So instead I give him a small nod and let him lift me from the floor.

"What's going on with my dad and the Cobras, Crow?" I ask. It's why I wanted to venture out today, to see if he knew anything.

"What do you mean?" He begins shifting uncomfortably at my question.

"He's been acting weird. I dunno, he's always out more and he won't tell me where he's going lately, which is unlike him. I know something is happening, everyone's always at the Club having meetings and no one will tell me anything. Is it about Gray? Have they found out who it was?" I know I could be wrong, but no one could find any solid proof around Gray's disappearance and although they suspected it was The Devils Henchmen, a rival motorcycle club, no one could do anything without some sort of proof without causing uproar and chaos.

"You know I can't tell you anything, Char. You know I would if I could, but I just can't risk it." So there is something going on. There must be or he would just tell me there was nothing.

"Can you at least tell me if it's about Gray? He's my brother, I deserve to know." Crow knows how much Gray's disappearance has affected me.

He rubs at the back of his neck, sighing before turning back to me.

"They don't know where he is, but they have someone who might. That's all I can say, alright? I shouldn't even be telling you that. You know your dad would skin me alive for telling you anything, Char." I know he's right, that no matter how much my dad adores Crow, he doesn't want me involved or knowing anything more than the essentials, the bare minimum.

"I know. I know you telling me anything is a risk and I'm sorry to ask but thank you, thank you for telling me." I appreciate it more than he could possibly know.

I pick up my tin, the flask, and empty cups before placing them in my backpack and closing the zip. I put the backpack straps over my shoulders, on top of Crow's jacket, and began the walk back home with him.

"I can't tell you what but there is something your dad is planning on approaching you about though, Char. Not Gray, but something I need you to think very carefully about before you commit. Do you understand?"

"Not even a little bit, no. What is it?" I wonder.

Crow doesn't say a word, just sighs and shakes his head as he puts his hand on my lower back and tells me we should go.

"Well? What do I need to think very carefully about?" I ask lightly as I echo his serious tone.

"You have to swear to me you won't say anything, Char, and I mean it. I'm only telling you because I think it's a shit idea and I think you have the right to have the heads up about it."

I nod my head, apprehensive suddenly, nervous. Crow is very rarely this sceptical or serious.

"They're talking about merging with The Laidens," he says as we continue to walk. He takes my hand in his, rubbing my palm with his fingers.

The Laidens are a motorcycle club not far from us. There are often tense ties between clubs and although there are very loose connections between the Laidens and The Dark Cobras, from what I can gather it seems they have been trying to join bands for a while.

"OK, but that has nothing to do with me."

"It could have everything to do with you if you marry their president's son." Crows voice comes out quiet, yet cold as ice, similarly to how the pit within my stomach drops as every ounce of blood within me freezes.

"Marriage? What are you talking about?" I rush out as I stop mid-step and turn to Crow, grabbing hold of his arm as he halts and sighs before finally turning to look at me.

"You can't tell him I've told you, Char, but that's the offer. You marry the son and the clubs merge." His words hit me like a tonne of bricks, knocking the oxygen out of my constricting lungs.

"There's no chance of a merge without that?" I question.

"No. Your dad tried every possible angle he could think of but they're insistent that the only way to truly merge and stand as one against The Devil's Henchmen and The Enforcers is to truly tie us all as one."

The Devil's Henchmen and The Enforcers. I remember thinking what stupid names they were for motorcycle clubs when I heard them as a child; and yet, now all I feel when hearing the names is dread.

We have two rival clubs determined to see us drown in our own blood, and we have no way of beating them without help. We need the help but I desperately want out of this life and love so much more.

Two

"Crow, will you turn the heating up for me?" I call behind me as I walk into the kitchen.

Our home is my reserve space, modest in its size and littered with old furniture that has been around for as long as I can remember. We're not really the type of people to update things or buy new unless it's really needed, and our home is perfectly rustic because of it.

I'm still reeling from Crow's revelation about the marriage pact that The Laidens have offered my dad. A large part of me is unsure if he would even approach me and ask such a thing of me, but then I know how much the Club and The Cobras mean to him. I know he would do anything for them, but does that include sacrificing his child's happiness?

I'm not even sure I want to get married, let alone anytime soon. I mean, I probably will get married one day, but to someone I love, someone that I have spent time getting to know, not a stranger that will tie me to Club life forever.

"Do you think your dad will mind if I stay again? I hate going to the Club to sleep." I wipe the thoughts of marriage from my mind and turn to Crow. Crow is always moaning about the Club house.

It's a nightclub, with rooms upstairs used as a hotel for our crew whenever they need it, a bar downstairs, a cafe in the day, a meeting ground, a place that manages to transform into whatever is needed really.

Crow doesn't like the girls that hang out there. The girls are usually after anyone with status. A lot of them are lovely, but there are a few that are only there because of the rumours they have heard and their incessant obsession over being with a 'bad boy'. It doesn't really work that way, not only because the Club is nothing like what the outside world perceives it to be, but also because most of the men there either have wonderful wives they would never waver from or simply aren't interested in girls, nor women that want them for anything other than them - but that's something many of the girls don't understand.

Crow doesn't want the women there and he can't stand the men fighting for their masculinity every time someone looks at them the wrong way. They aren't all like that, it's more often than not the younger members and prospects that feel they need to earn their way in through fighting.

"You know he won't mind, you're here all the time, you're like a son to him, Crow. Don't stress," I tell him as I collect the mince from the fridge and the potatoes ready to start peeling and cooking.

Crow sits down on one of the chairs at the table in the middle of the kitchen. He gets his phone out and scrolls aimlessly through Facebook, Twitter, Snapchat, or whatever other app he can find to amuse himself with.

The one thing I've wondered about since he came around is how he ever finds time to do anything, have friends, girlfriends, or let loose if he's always with me.

The idea of him having a girlfriend makes me cringe. Though he's not been with a girl that I know of since we've been around one another, I know the day will inevitably come if I never make a move or confess to the brewing feelings I have for him. Hell, even then it may still happen if he doesn't feel the same way.

I guess he must be okay with the lack of time away though. Even if he wouldn't say anything to Dad, he would have said something to me by now if it was something that bothered him.

"Are you coming with us to collect Liam next week?" Crow asks me. He hasn't met Liam before since he's not long joined and found his way up the ranks when he had the job of looking after me assigned to him.

"What do you want to know about him?" I ask with a chuckle.

He's not interested in if I'll be there. He's only interested in finding out what Liam's going to be like as the president. He's never seen anyone apart from my dad as President and a new one can change things drastically, although I know that won't happen. Well, I hope it won't.

Liam and Dad have been friends since my dad was ten years old. Liam and my dad were still young when he got sent down, and I was only eight myself. I remember him being there all the time, living with me and Dad because he didn't have any family, or a partner to go home to, and since my mum left when I was only four, my dad raised me, and Liam sat on the sidelines as the uncle that was never really my uncle.

"What's he like? Do you think he'll get rid of us lot?" Crow wonders.

He's hesitant, as are most of the new members that have never met him. They've all been told the stories about him. He's ruthless, filled with anger, willing to kill if you breathe wrong and fiercely closed in on himself. From what I remember, most of them are just stories though, or at the very least exaggerated stories based on small sections of truth.

The stories about him are endless. One of the newer prospects told me one last week that he had heard. Apparently Liam had beaten ten men by himself, all because they walked into his club and didn't leave a tip for the bartender who had put up with their egotistical bullshit all night. Every time someone tells it, they add a little bit more to the story, meaning that at this stage I'm pretty certain it's a complete lie.

Having grown up with him for eight years of my life, and through the phone calls that took place when he first got locked up until I was thirteen and no longer had any interest in talking to my dad's friends, and would much rather see or speak to my own instead, I know more about him than a lot of the men and women that will soon be under his control. So, I give in and I tell Crow what I know. Which isn't really much of anything considering I only know of Liam what I witnessed through a child's mind.

"He always used to be pretty hard faced, but fair." I take a breath, thinking of the times he would reprimand me as a child but was never cruel. "Strict, but understanding..." I pause again. "Undeniably and fiercely protective of those he's loyal to and those that are loyal to him," I tell Crow. "But then I don't have a clue what he's like now. Other than shouting hello when Dad's been on the phone to him, I've not spoken to or seen him in years."

I think back to all of the summers throughout my childhood when Liam would take me to the park if Dad was busy with club business and watch over me as if the world stopped and started with my ability to be happy and carefree. Dad always says that Liam had a terrible life before he joined the club and that's why he always made sure that I was happy, because watching a child be born into the same dynamic that he was made him want a different life for me than the one he had growing up.

"Your dad wouldn't let him get rid of us all, would he?" Crow wonders as he sits fidgeting with his hands and the ends of the sleeve jacket. He's nervous.

"You know my dad speaks to him on the phone every week, he tells him everything he's done, and Liam's happy with it. He believes in my dad and has had just as much of a say as Dad has in bringing new people into the club, Crow. Don't worry, I promise, you'll be fine," I tell him.

I turn back around and continue on with the cooking that I had started. I can understand why he's concerned. I'm anxious to see him and to find out what changes he plans to make, if any at all. No matter how much he trusts my dad and his judgement, things are bound to alter. I just hope it doesn't negatively affect Crow. Or me, for that matter.

Crow didn't have a home or a family that loved him when he joined us. He wouldn't have anywhere to go if he got kicked out.

"Not as though you will be, but you know that even if you were kicked out that I'd come with you, Crow. You can come with me to uni, or we could find somewhere of our own," I tell him with a smile as I turn around and notice him giving me what is one of his most genuine smiles. It's warm, honest, and everything that this world isn't. Crow's a pure man, no matter what he's done under orders of the club. Crow's good.

"I wish it were that simple, Char. There are things at play that no one even knows about."

"What do you mean? What hands are at play?" Is he talking about The Devil's Henchmen? Does he know something? Or is it the marriage, or even Gray? With the way things are going lately, it could be just about anything that he's referring to.

I put the food in the oven and take a seat next to Crow.

"I wish I could tell you, but just know that there's more happening around us than I think anyone here realises." He knows something about the Club that he's not telling me. If he can't tell me, I need to make sure that Dad does. And if he won't then I'll just have to find out for myself.

I hear the door open and close as the scent of diesel comes into the house. My dad. He's a mechanic by trade and although there are other mechanics within the ranks of the Cobras, my dad likes to work on his bike himself.

"You two alright?" my dad shouts through to us as he takes off his boots in the hall.

"Yeah, just making tea," I yell back at him.

"Can I have a word with you before tea, Charlie darlin'?" He says it so casually, with no hint of worry or uncertainty.

I know what it is. Thanks to Crow.

Crow and I exchange a look before I nod at my dad, telling Crow to keep an eye on the food as I follow my dad through to his study.

My dad's study is rather bare, consisting of his desk with a plush chair behind it and one in front of the desk. The only other items in the room are filing cabinets and a few pictures scattered around the place.

I take a seat at the chair on the opposite side of the desk to my dad and wait while he gets a glass and fills it with whiskey. I can't stand the stuff.

He takes a sip before turning to face me.

"You know we want to join with The Laidens, don't you?" He hasn't told me that himself but he knows I'm privy to Cobra gossip and talk when in the Clubhouse. He's aware that I know a lot through others even if he doesn't like it.

I nod, not saying a word, knowing exactly where this conversation is heading.

He nods at me and takes another sip before putting his glass down on the desk in front of him and clasping his hands together.

"They've offered us a merge."

"Well, that's good, isn't it?" I ask, knowing it's very well not a good thing considering the stipulation they've added to the merge taking place.

"Yeah, yeah it is but they'll only merge if we do something for them."

Here it comes.

"They want you to marry the president's son, darlin." The

words are said steadily, with little to no emotion behind them. He's attempting to gauge my reaction, as I am his.

I make sure to widen my eyes and sit forwards in my seat, at least attempting to feign shock even though I already know what he's telling me.

"And you told them no, I assume." It's not a question, though it should be and it's one I want answered anyway.

My dad shifts in his seat uncomfortably before facing me again.

"Well, here's the thing, Charlie darlin', you're a grown woman now. You'll be getting married at some time anyway, I have no doubt, and if it can benefit the family then I, I'd like you to think about it." He looks sheepish and so he should.

I truly thought he wouldn't dare ask me. That he wouldn't even question it and yet he did. He is. He wants me to do it.

"Benefit the family? Dad, you've never wanted me involved in Club life and now you want me to marry into it and to a stranger?" I practically yell.

I can feel myself getting worked up, angry, frustrated at the lack of care he's showing. He doesn't seem phased at all by any of this, and yet it was only a few weeks ago that he was ranting at me for wanting to be involved.

"I can't and won't force you, but you know what's at stake here, I don't have to tell you. They may even be able to help us find Gray." That's what this is. He's trading me in for the hope of finding Gray.

I want to find Gray more than anything in the world and he knows that. Everyone knows that, but surely there is another way. There has to be another way.

"That's a low blow and you know it," I hiss at him as I get up and leave.

"I've set up a meeting with the son, so you can get to know each other. Day after tomorrow." His face is unforgiving, completely void of emotion. So unlike the man that he's been up until this very moment.

"You didn't even wait for me to say yes?"

He doesn't respond and with my hand on the doorknob, I find an idea entering my mind.

"I'm not a virgin, you know. That's what he'll want, isn't it? He won't want damaged goods." I lie. I am a virgin, but if pretending I'm not will cancel this ridiculous set up then I'm all for spending the rest of my life covered in the web of lies I can create.

He winces at my words, the first show of any feeling since this conversation started.

"He doesn't care about that. And I really don't want to know about that, Charlie, but since when have you been around anyone without me or Crow or Gray long enough for that to happen? Jesus, darlin'." I roll my eyes at his berating tone.

As if right now is the time for that conversation. Not as though there's even a conversation to be had about my fake loss of virginity.

"Oh, for fuck's sake, Dad, I didn't tell you that so that we can have the bloody bees and the birds talk again," I tell him with a sigh.

"Fine, but just meet him. Please. He'll be at the Club, somewhere comfortable for you. His idea." He says it as if I should be grateful to the man that is trying to steal my right to choose.

Fucking men.

Three

Crow and I fell asleep together watching some documentary on Netflix last night. As I wake up to the sun shining through my cream curtains, I look to my right and see that Crow is still sleeping soundly. I fell asleep in my fluffy teddy bear pyjamas, long pyjama bottoms and a flannel fluffy top. Crow's in his boxer shorts as usual. He fell asleep on top of my duvet. Dad must have come in to check on us at some point, because Crow's now got a light blanket on top of him.

Dad is normally adamant that I don't even speak to men, which is ironic really considering he's currently trying to marry me off, but when it comes to this heavy sleeper next to me, I think he has a soft spot for him. Even though I'm Crow's assignment to protect, Dad knows that he means more to me than just that.

I watch Crow for a few minutes, taking in the abs any guy would kill for, his tanned skin that never seems to pale, even in the adverse weather we seem to be having this winter. He always looks like he's just been on holiday somewhere warm. He has skin that's so blemish free it's easy to imagine him on a magazine cover.

I put my bare feet to the ground and as they rest on the warmth of the carpet below my bed, I look to my left, towards one of the two double windows in my room, and spot the clock on my bedside table: 6.09am. It's no wonder the house is still so eerily silent.

I groggily wipe my face and clamber from the bed gently, careful not to wake the now sleeping and snoring man next to me, and find myself in front of my dresser, picking out some dark denim skinny jeans and one of Gray's black hoodies out of my drawer that makes me look tiny. It's ridiculously baggy, but I like the fact that it overwhelms my body and I love that it's my brother's.

I used to like wearing Gray's dressing gowns, jumpers, and jackets when I was little just to wind him up. I loved that he never objected even though they were practically dresses on me. Now they serve as a reminder of Gray.

I made a list of the ways I could attempt to find him. I just need to make sure that no one knows what I am attempting. Despite his recent very abrupt change of mind about me being involved in Club life, I know my dad will still object to me doing anything that will endanger myself in order to find Gray.

I shake my head in an attempt to wash away the thoughts of Gray for now and wander into the en-suite attached to my bedroom and quickly strip out of my pyjamas before jumping into the warmth of the shower. I ease my head back as I let the water trickle over my face and down my chest and into the abyss of the plughole at the bottom of the bathtub that my shower head hangs above.

It doesn't take me long to shower, wash my hair, clean myself, brush my teeth, and get dressed again before opening the door and leaving the steaming room behind.

I towel dry my hair before untangling it with my trusted *Game Of Thrones* brush that Crow got me for Christmas, throw the towel into the laundry basket, and pad quietly out of my bedroom door and down the stairs, careful not to wake

21

anyone. I unlock and open the front door and sit on the steps in front of my house.

As I sit and look out at the houses around ours, their occupants beginning to wake up and start their day, I think about what my plans are.

I need to go shopping in town with Crow and decorate Liam's old room so that it's ready for him to come home to. He'll be moving back in with us. You would have thought he would want a place of his own, so that he could bring women back, or have meetings in, or do whatever it is that he wants once he's free, but when Dad asked him, he had apparently said he couldn't live away from us. God knows why, he hadn't lived with us for years and we're not very exciting, but that's his mistake, I guess. Maybe that's what he wants though, away from the chaos of club life, maybe he just wants some normality, much like Crow I suppose.

I remember suddenly that I'll also need to wake Crow soon, so that we can get into town and back before we're expected at the clubhouse for two pm. Dad has got some work for us. Well, for Crow but Crow and I are inseparable so I tend to go with him to the Club whenever he's needed there.

It seems so absurd to be spending the morning and potentially the rest of the weekend decorating a room for someone I haven't seen in years when I have a brother that's missing and a potential forced marriage to contend with.

I wonder how Gray would handle this. What he would do or say. I knew he wouldn't stand for it and although part of me wants to completely ignore the meeting my dad has set up, I know that for the sake of Gray and hopefully gaining information, I have to at least meet the man that my father seems intent on pawning me off to.

As much as I want to find him myself, since no one will let me help, I have very little to go on.

It is so out of character for Dad that I am curious how the Laidens had even got him to come round to the idea. He was hesitant about putting Crow with me at the beginning, simply because Crow was a man; and now here he is, willing and even encouraging the idea of me marrying someone I have never even met.

Dad has always done his best to keep me out of the areas of the Cobra life that he deems too much for me. He doesn't involve me in it too much and I don't ask. Any time I ever dare to question it, he tells me I'm being silly, that nothing illegal goes on, but I highly suspect that's a lie.

I've become more and more inquisitive since Gray's disappearance. I know he was involved with the Cobras and although he didn't tell me much, he told me enough for me to know that there is a lot more going on than what Dad would have me know.

I notice Tin and Dove walking towards the house.

"What are you two old fuckers doing up this early?" I shout down at them as they begin to climb the stairs to our front door.

They both chuckle at me, and Tin, one of the Club's counsellors and a close friend of my dad's, lands next to me in a sitting position, with his legs outstretched onto the steps before him. Dove scoots round him, putting a hand on my hair and ruffling it up as he always does when he sees me.

"We're here for breakfast, you little sod." Dove laughs as he talks to me, shaking his head as he opens the front door of the house to go and start breakfast. They come around most mornings. Neither of them have partners or kids so they spend a lot of their time here.

When I look next to me and see Tin sitting there, I notice that he's now smoking alongside me.

"Couldn't sleep or just missed this beautiful face?" I ask as he blows out the smoke inhibiting its space in his lungs.

Tin smirks and knocks my shoulder with his.

"Well, hell, little lady, you can't be beating on me this early in the morning." Tins voice is gruff, though his words are anything but.

As well as Liam, both Tin and Dove have been around since before I was born. Tin, Liam, and Dove aren't the longest standing men in the club by any means, but they are the ones that are closest to my dad and I.

~

"Where are we going then? Or am I just driving aimlessly for a while?" Crow asks me.

He's driving, as always. I have my driving license but I can daydream when someone else is driving and the last time I started daydreaming when I drove, I nearly crashed, not as though I told anyone that. I don't even seem to notice when my mind takes off to a different dimension. Trying to pay attention and drive alongside it does not go well.

"Okay, we need to go to B&M first, we'll see what we can find in there," I declare as I close the book in my lap before tucking it neatly into my backpack.

"I think we're going to go with neutral colours for him, you think that'll be ok?" I ask eagerly, not wanting to mess up, but needing a man's view, because no matter how much I know about men, which isn't much at all really, I'm not sure I'm quite on par with what a nearly forty-year-old bloke is going to want in his bedroom.

"You do remember that I haven't met him, right? I haven't got a clue what he'd want, Char," he tells me as his eyes scan every mirror the car has for signs of danger behind us.

I notice that Crow does this constantly. The reason I notice is because I do it too. We've both been taught, although through very different means admittedly, to constantly keep an eye out for danger and being the daughter of the man in charge of a motorcycle club invites danger, meaning that both Crow and I are constantly on the lookout.

There have been so many times I've been followed, it's only natural to be paranoid. Paranoia's horrible but it keeps you safe most of the time, so I don't mind it.

"Grey's a safe colour though. Can't go wrong with grey." Crow interrupts my thoughts, and as I look at him, I find that he's got his coffee in his left hand whilst he uses his right to steer.

Grey's safe.

"We gonna get some lunch after this shit show of a shopping trip, Char? I'm hungry already," Crow whines. He's like some crazed dog, he doesn't stop eating and acts like it's both the first time he's ever seen the food and the last time he ever will each time he has a meal.

"You're such a pig. You ate an hour ago, for God's sake, and what do you mean shit show of a shopping trip? We haven't even got inside yet!" I tell him as he parks up in a bay space and opens his door.

I follow his lead and head out of his white Golf, slamming the door shut behind me. I walk round the front of the car towards Crow and start off towards the front doors of B&M.

"I might have ate an hour ago, but if you fed me bigger meals, then I wouldn't be hungry all the time and no, but I hate shopping, so it's bound to be bad." I can't help but scoff at this, he had the biggest breakfast out of everyone and made a mess of the table in my kitchen in the process. I do admittedly know that he hates shopping though so I give him credit for not giving me too much of a hard time about dragging him along.

"Oh, stop moaning and follow me, you big baby."

I collect a trolley from outside of the shop and head in, going straight for the home aisle.

I pick up a grey and white patterned double duvet cover and throw it in the trolley straight away, paying little attention to the phone-obsessed Crow behind me. He's staring down at the little screen as if it holds his whole life that he just can't help but look at.

25

There are two dark grey lamps, a floor lamp that's as tall as me and a small one you touch to activate. I stare at them both, figuring out which would go best before deciding to pick them both up and moving along. I collect matching bathroom accessories, pillows for atop of the bed, some floating shelves, a couple of photo frames, and a rug before turning down the next aisle in search of the perfect shade of paint.

Egg green? Stained ivory? Ion blue? Translucent Grey? Crayon yellow? Holy hell, can't they just have simplistic terms for colours and shades rather than about fifty different shades for each colour? I decide on a magnolia, duck grey, and vase grey (basically light and dark grey, whoever decides the names of these things just has a problem that can't be solved).

Now to see how good my decorating skills are when I put it all together in Liam's room.

"You took forever," Crow tells me as we head back towards the car.

"I was less than half an hour in there! You should be grateful, I could always decide I want to go clothes shopping too," I declare.

"You wouldn't dare."

"Oh you know I would but luckily for you, I'm not feeling it today," I tell him with a smirk. I hate clothes shopping, but he doesn't need to know that.

"Get in the car." Crows voice is as cold as ice as he opens the door and shoves me in.

"Excuse me bu"- My words are cut off as I realise what or rather who he's eyeing up. I open the door, my hand on the back of his leather jacket.

Edgar is heading our way with a group of the Devil's Dealers not far behind him. He's the President's son, formidable in his appearance with dark, soulless eyes and a very nearly bald head that shows off the scar running across his forehead and the burns covering his head, cheek and upper chest, as well as the countless tattoos plastered along his bare forearms.

I watch on as Crow is facing the gruesome bunch of men that head our way.

My dad had always taught me that although fear can often be useful, it's letting fear overwhelm you that puts you in danger. Right now, it feels like I'm being overwhelmed by fear.

They haven't done anything threatening, but I know them. I know they went after Gray, whether there's any proof or not. I'm certain of it. They are the only rival Club that would have enough gall to go directly after a member, let alone the President's son.

I know what they're capable of from the stories I've heard and unlike the ones I've heard about Liam that I have no doubt are mostly false, the stories about these men come from the men within the Cobras that have seen the torture they inflict first-hand.

"What do you want, Edgar?" Crow often acts grumpy or illusive around others but this isn't him acting. He isn't just grumpy, he's uptight, angry, and ready to attack. You can see it in the stance he's holding, legs wide, hands clenched.

"Princess not coming out to say hello?" Edgar asks with a laugh as those with him follow along and laugh at his seriously unfunny joke.

Crow takes a few steps away from me, closer to them.

I hate Crow being so close to them alone. I know he can handle himself but there are six of them and only one of him. Despite how well trained he may be, those aren't great odds.

"I just wanted to come and say hello to the princess. The last time I saw her in person, she was a small wee thing. She's practically prime for fucking now. I can imagine now just how sweet she'd be to break." His words come out with a smile so hollow it's hard to imagine any woman willingly going near him.

His words make me cringe in disgust, knowing all of the awful things he's done to women in his time. So many of the women he's hurt are now protected by the Dark Cobras.

Crow inches closer to Edgar, his face taking on a look of pure fury.

"You even think about her again, and I will crush you and every one of these pussy ass sheep that follow you. Do you understand me?" His words are low, quiet yet no less threatening.

Edgar looks from me to Crow, looking him up and down before returning his eyes to me.

"I'm only playing with you. No one wants a marked girl. Not worth the hassle," he says with a dry laugh.

"What the fuck do you mean marked?" Crow growls at him.

"You haven't heard? She's for sale. Marked. Bet dear Daddy is the one that's got her up there. Always did think he was a bit dark for the Cobras with his taste for pain. Do say hello to the dear ol' Pres for me, won't you, princess?" He speaks without taking his eyes off me. I feel disgusting. My mind goes blank when I register what he's said. Marked? Questions are racing around my mind as Edgar walks off with his trail of men eagerly following behind him.

Crow gets in the car and starts driving without saying a word.

"What did he mean, Crow? How am I marked? For sale. I can't be, can I?" I ask him.

I know what it means and so does Crow. So many of the other MC clubs not only in the country but around the world sell, trade, and deal with human trafficking – women, men, children. To be marked means that you have a price on your head, that you've been marked and put on the black market for sale.

"I don't know." His words are short, abrupt, the edge to his voice like steel.

"What do you mean you don't know? You must know something, Crow! What was he talking about? He must be wrong." Even if it is about me, I know Dad won't tell me anything. Someone must know.

28

I couldn't be for sale. That's impossible. Who would put me up for sale? You need pictures, a trafficking passport, and who knows what else to even mark someone. I immediately dismiss his suggestion about my dad. No matter who my dad is when I'm not around, I know that he loves me. No matter what, I know he will never do anything to put me in danger.

The marriage pops into my mind, and although I've spent the time since he told me questioning his moral compass, I know for certain that he wouldn't do that unless he felt it would keep me safe. Maybe that's what it is, he does know about me being marked and that's why he wants the Laidens and The Cobras to merge. It means more protection and finding Gray.

"I need to make a phone call. Do not say a word. Not a single word, do you understand me?" I nod numbly at Crow's words.

Crow pressed some buttons on the screen in front of us and within two rings, a voice I don't recognise answers.

"Down Viper Swing." What the hell?

"Viper Whiskey Spring," Crow replies cryptically.

What on earth is going on? Are we reciting in rhyme? I can rhyme plenty, I'm just not sure this is the time somehow.

"Take her off the register. Now."

"I can't, man. I wish I could, but it's out of my hands. The Lopezs have put her on there," the strange voice says.

"Down Viper Spring." Crow hangs up.

Who were the Lopezs? I haven't heard that name before. If it isn't The Devil's Dealers that have done this as some kind of way to antagonise my dad into starting a war between the Clubs as I had first assumed, and it was instead these Lopezs, then I need to find out who they are and why they are after me.

"Who was that?" I ask Crow.

"Some computer whizz the Cobras have contact with. I was hoping he'd be able to get onto the market and get you off it."

"Who are the Lopezs? Are they worse than the Dealers?"

"FUCK!" The roar that comes from Crow as he punches

29

the steering wheel scares me. It's guttural and filled with fury unlike anything I've seen him express before.

You would think that having lived the life I have that not much would scare me anymore, but the unhinged anger coming from Crow is unlike anything I've ever seen him showing. I've seen him mad, angry, frustrated--but never like this. His hands are shaking and his jaw is clenched as he stares at the road ahead.

I put my hand on his, gently so as not to startle him. His jawline ticks but he doesn't take his eyes off the road or acknowledge that I've touched him.

Eventually, he takes his left hand off the wheel and intertwines his fingers with mine, using his thumb to rub the topside of my hand.

"I just need you to be ok, Char."

Four

I am sitting at the bar in the clubhouse. It is always busy at this time of day, filled with workers and the public alike. In the day, it's a cafe, with sofa chairs and tables accompanying them. The atmosphere is more laid back, with club members milling around, either chowing down on lunch or goofing off, waiting for something to happen.

I am sitting, chatting to one of the barmaids, Alice, when Crow walks in searching for me.

Alice brushes her hair down and starts twisting a strand with her hand. She's had a thing for Crow for far too long without either him noticing or her telling him. It is never ending with them two - Crow is clueless, and Alice is shy. She has never outright told me that she likes him, but it is clear that she does.

Crow takes the seat next to me and immediately starts on the food I ordered for him. I got him a double cheeseburger and chips. He told me to order food whilst he was on the phone outside and without telling me what he wanted, burger and chips is the safest option. He doesn't seem to mind, wolfing it down as though he's not eaten in days.

"Do you know what's going on around here today? Everyone is acting super skittish," Alice tells us as she eyes the men around us.

There do seem to be more Cobras around than usual and unlike normal, they're not sitting drinking or relaxing. They're on guard - alert. I wonder silently if it has anything to do with my marking and Edgar's appearance earlier but realise that Crow didn't call anyone and inform them apart from the nameless computer whizz. Maybe whoever that was had contacted everyone else.

"I have no idea. You know more than I do around here. Has anyone said anything?" I ask her.

It's the truth about her knowing more than me. Alice has been around for a few years. She doesn't dance like a lot of the girls, she instead prefers to bartend or waitress, meaning that she often overhears a lot more than what the Cobras realise. It is through Alice that I get information that no one else wants to freely give me. She's about the same height as me, though a few years older. Alice is bigger in build than I am; curvy and constantly hyper and smiley. She is beautiful.

"No, nothing," she squeaks out, looking right at Crow, who is paying little to no attention to our conversation.

"Keep your eyes open and your ears peeled. I have a feeling you'll be hearing your fair share soon enough," I tell her, and notice Crow's look of annoyance at me as I do.

Crow knows I get most of the information I know about the Club from her, but he doesn't say anything to either one of us as he rolls his eyes and continues on with his food.

"Hey, Crow, have you spoken to Dad?" I ask, and as slowly as he does anything that he has little interest in, he raises his head to look Alice over quickly before looking at me again and nodding, all the while still munching on his burger.

"Yeah, I called him before. He's on his way," he gets out, barely understandable with the food in his mouth.

Before I get a chance to say anymore, my dad's behind me; I can feel his presence before he says a thing.

I turn around instinctually and my eyes fall on my father. He's a tall man, a little taller than Crow, although only by an inch or so, but the way he carries himself makes him look seven feet tall. He has pitch black hair, his is as straight as rods, whereas mine waves in annoying curls. He needs a haircut, I note as he smiles at me.

"You coming with us, my darling Charlie?" he asks.

So we're pretending as if he isn't pawning me off now? I can do that.

"If Crow's there then so am I, gotta protect the poor fellow, haven't I?" I joke as Crow glances at me in frustration.

I don't mention Edgar or what he said. He wouldn't answer me anyway, so I certainly don't plan on asking in front of anyone and embarrassing myself by letting everyone hear him treat me like a child and refuse to tell me anything.

Crow hates when I talk about protecting him. Even though that's exactly what I hope I'd be able to do if it ever came to it. Even though I know how capable he is, I know I would do anything for him, including attempt and fail to stick up for him.

"Alright, come on then, kids. The men are waiting," my dad tells us before rubbing my back and turning on his heel as he heads towards the stairs. We're going to the basement, I'm sure of it. The stairs lead upstairs to the bedrooms, or down stairs to the basement, and I have no reason to believe the men are waiting for us in the hotel rooms, so basement it is. Shit.

I turn to look at Crow as he soon realises the same thing that I have. They want Crow to do something bad.

It's sort of like an initiation. One that Crow has failed three times already. He never tells me exactly what he has to do, but he does tell me that he hasn't done what he was supposed to. And considering he's supposed to protect me, that's a problem, or at least for Dad it is. Fuck. They aren't going to give him

33

many more chances if he can't do it today. If he goes, I go too, I decide. I meant what I told him about leaving together.

"You can come back for your burger later, boy, let's go!" my dad shouts back at us as he nears the stairs at the complete opposite end of the room to us.

Crow and I get up together and start after my dad.

"It's fine, you'll be fine, Crow," I tell him, even though as much as I hate not believing in him, I'm not convinced my words are true.

"Don't bullshit me, Char. I can't fucking do it and you know it," he tells me.

I take hold of his hand and give it a little squeeze. I don't know how else to support him.

As we eventually enter the basement, it makes sense why it needs to be soundproof. I can hear shouting from the cells and grunts coming from the one room now in use.

Dad's holding the door open for us as we walk in. He doesn't usually let me get this far, but I refuse to speak up and remind him of that fact. Any morsels of information he's allowing me to have, I'm taking.

I recognise the man sitting in the chair. He's from one of the other clubs, I'm sure of it. I close my eyes briefly in frustration, knowing that whatever comes can't be good.

I note that I'm still holding onto Crow's hand so let go gently, not wanting to startle him or allow for anyone else to notice. I don't care if they see, but they'll see my comforting him as a weakness for Crow.

Dad stands next to the man who's bloody and bruised, and looks straight ahead at Crow and I.

"This man helped orchestrate the attack on us. He has given us the information we need, though there's one more thing we'd like to know." My dad looks at me as he says this. He wants me to know, to understand.

"I'd like you to leave now, Charlie darlin. You can wait outside," my dad tells me.

I can see Crow shaking, though I bet no one else notices that part. They're too hungry for this mans blood.

Fuck, fuck, fuck.

My dad comes towards us, pushing me gently towards the door.

It's only then as I turn to whisper words of comfort to Crow that I notice the man doesn't have anything covering his mouth and yet he's not said a word. Surely he should be angry and screaming, upset and frustrated and crying, pleading or begging or trying to get out of the chains in a last attempt to get free. Doing something. Anything.

This man is sitting perfectly still, watching and I'm sure assessing those around him. Mainly Crow as the new one in the room.

My dad nudges me to leave once more and the last thing I see before I do is the man in the chair, all bloodied and dirty watching me intently before smirking briefly at me as I walk out and mouthing three words when the others are too busy ushering me out to notice.

He'll get you.

The heavy metal door slams shut behind me. So I wait. Thinking over the mans words. *He'll get you.* The man is a member of a band of men that attacked the Club not so long ago. They call themselves The Enforcers. Even the name sounds ridiculous. The enforcers of what exactly? No one's going to get me. I continue to wait. And wait. What if he knows something about the marking? I anxiously wait a while more, unable to hear a thing going on inside the room behind me because of these stupid soundproof walls.

And then, as if nothing has happened and no time has passed, they're back and closing the door behind them.

"Son, I'm proud of what-"

I interrupted my dad, "Of what?"

"He's a part of us, now more than ever, Charlie, but we may need to swap him round with one of the other guys to watch you for a while." My dad eyes me dubiously, knowing just as well as I do what's about to come out of my mouth.

"I'm not having anyone follow me around, Dad – well, not unless it's Crow. Considering I'm currently marked, up for sale, Gray's gone, and we have The Enforcers and The Devil's Dealers around trying to constantly find a reason for a war, the safest thing is for me to be with someone I trust, Dad, and that person is Crow. Please, please don't have someone else do it," I beg him.

"Char, it's only one day a week. That's all and I promise you, no one will get to you. Not the Enforcers or the Dealers," Dad tells me.

Crow says nothing, but he nods, slightly, only slightly at my dad who eyes him cautiously.

"What's going on? What don't I know now?" I ask in frustration.

I don't move beside Crow. I watch as he once again eyes my father, waiting for him to speak.

"Charlie darlin', there's no way you're able to go to the city next weekend to see Nina. It's too dangerous at the moment," my dad tells me.

In all the chaos and unrest that's been happening the last few days, I had completely forgotten about going to see Nina.

Nina has been my best friend throughout high school and when she went off to University in Cardiff, I had promised to go and stay with her once a month for the weekend which up until now I have done, but I understand that my dad is right. Between Gray's disappearance, the mark on me, and the rival gangs gaining on us, it is too much of a risk. Not just to me, but to Nina as well if anyone catches me with her and uses her as leverage.

"OK. I get it, I'll have the new guard one day a week, I won't go to Nina's, but I need you to tell me what's going on. I feel like my head is going to explode, Dad," I tell him, feeling exhausted from the constant mismatch of thoughts going on in my head.

"Charlie, I'm sorry, but the less you know the better. You know this."

"No, I don't, Dad. This is about me! And Gray, and no matter how much you don't want me involved, I already am just by being your daughter." He winces at my words, knowing that no matter how hard it is to hear that it's the truth.

"It's not as simple as you think it is, darlin'. Look, I've got to go. There's a meeting here tomorrow, one that you should be here for, as you well know, and I need to make sure everything is ready. I'll see you at home," he tells me just as Tin walks up to us.

"Me and Crow are going to finish our food now," I declare as I take Crow's hand to leave.

"Is it bad? I mean, really that bad?" I ask quietly as we walk away from my dad and Tin.

"I'll protect you, I swear I will." Crows words affect me more than I'd like to admit. Not only because him saying that means that it really is that bad but because if it is that bad then I'm just as worried about him as I am about myself.

And then I have an idea.

"What did you have to do earlier? That you couldn't do before, what is it you had to do?" I ask him.

"You know I can't tell you that, Char. I wish you'd stop asking me to tell you things you know I can't. I don't want to hide things from you but I can't not," he tells me, looking as defeated as I felt only moments ago.

"But what if you could tell me? What if I was a Dark Cobra? You could then, right?" I ask eagerly.

Crow stops me, looks both ways to be sure there's no one around and then looks me dead in the eyes. He doesn't move for a moment, looking at me so intently I'm sure he's either in shock or thinks I'm delusional. Or maybe both.

"Do not ever let your dad hear you say that. In fact, just

don't ever say that again. You are not now, nor ever will you become, a Cobra."

"Why? It makes sense. I've been around the Dark Cobras my whole life, my dad is a Cobra, my brother was a recruit. Why can't I be one?"

"Women aren't Cobras, Char," he says as he drops his head.

"Why?! We're not in the twentieth century anymore, Crow, women can do just a-"

"It's nothing to do with what women can and can't do, Char. If women were Cobras then the men would automatically try and protect them, more so than they would the men around them. It's just automatic and if it's one of the men's wives or daughters then it's even more distracting because he will be spending every minute trying to protect her rather than doing his job. That leads to lives lost, problems caused and just – no. No, Char." He releases a breath, lets me go, and continues walking towards the cafe.

"What if you just train me up then so that I can look after myself? I won't mention the Cobras again, but at least if you help me train then I'll have a chance at protecting myself if I ever need to," I tell him with certainty.

"I thought your dad trained you and Gray," he says as we walk towards the bar and the seats we were previously sat at. Crow's food was still there. Untouched.

"Well, he did, but I've never put it to practise. I don't have a clue if I'd actually ever be able to use what he taught us. Learning in a room with people you know won't hurt you is very different to actually fighting off people that want to kill you. I mean, I imagine it is. I used to tell my dad to stop if I got tired, I don't think The Dealers or Enforcers will listen to me if I tell them to stop somehow," I tell him with raised eyebrows, knowing that he can't argue with that logic.

I think of all of the times Gray and I would spar as Dad watched on and encouraged us, telling us which way to dodge the other. He always used to tell me to use my size as an advantage over Gray, to be fast, nimble, and small was a good thing just like for Gray to be large, intimidating, and strong was a good thing.

"Fine. Tomorrow morning we'll start." I try and fail to hide the smile that's brewing as Crow rolls his eyes at my antics.

Five

"**Y**ou need to dodge me, Char. If you can't block then you at least need to dodge." We've been at it for an hour, and nothing I do seems to make me any better. I know having the skill to fight or defend yourself isn't something that can appear within an hour of training, but I think a small part of me hoped that my dad's training from when Gray and I were younger would kick in and I would at least be able to show Crow that I was capable of something. But no.

"I'm trying!" I yell at him as he comes for me again.

He keeps repeating the same actions over and over again. Backing away, coming at me again in different directions while I try to either block or dodge him. He seems to get me in a position I can't get out of every time though, no matter which way I go.

"Stop. Just stop. God, you're worse than I thought," he says with a laugh.

"Excuse me!" I exclaim, pissed off at his blunt nature. I mean, I know I'm bad, but no need to beat me while I'm down. Jeez.

"You've got to show me something here. What can you do?"

"I can punch. Dad always used to say I could throw a good punch."

Crow eyes me curiously.

"Fine. Maybe I've been going at this all wrong just trying to get you to defend. Maybe you'd be better off attacking," he says, walking towards me.

"Hit me."

"What, n-" He interrupts me with a hard look.

"I can't just hit you, Crow," I tell him.

"Afraid you'll hurt me?" He laughs.

"Well yeah!" I tell him, watching as he walks around me. He's circling me.

I can't keep my eyes away from him. He's just in his shorts and even though I've seen him in his shorts and boxers a million times, all I can think about is how his muscles ripple and move every time he moves. He has the body of a god and although there are plenty of things I would love to do to him, hitting him is not one of them.

"Hit me or I won't train you anymore," he tells me seriously, straight faced, as he pulls to a stop in front of me.

I need him to train me. Dad won't teach me anything anymore insisting that I don't need it and although I hope like hell that he's right, if he's not and I ever do end up in a situation where I need to fight my way out, I would currently be completely and utterly screwed.

I have power behind my punches, I know that much.

"Fine, but I can't just hit you stood there like that. You need to hit me or come at me or something. I just can't otherwise."

Crow smirks deliciously at me as he walks away and then spins and is running towards me too quickly for me to think about what I do before I do it.

I launch my body towards him, my right arm extending straight towards his face, landing below his chin as I push my weight up with my fist. Crows eyes looked as shocked as I feel as he staggers backwards and his head lolls to the side.

"Fuck, Char!" he yells as he rubs his chin and shakes his head at me.

"You said to hit you!" I scream, unable to stop the way my voice raises at both his outburst and the shock from actually hitting him. I can't believe I just hit him straight in the face. Oh god, I knew I shouldn't have bloody hit him. Why didn't I just go for his shoulder or something?

"That was hard! I said hit me not try and fucking knock me out! Jesus fucking Christ, woman!"

"Oh fucking hell, let me look at it," I tell him as I walk towards him, realising in hindsight that I probably should have avoided his face because now my dad will be extra curious as to what the hell is going on If I've managed to bruise him.

"Why didn't you tell me earlier that you could punch? We've wasted an hour on self defence. If I knew you could hit like that, I'd have started there from the off," he tells me.

"I don't know, I didn't think. Let me see your face."

"Why is your lip bleeding? I didn't hit your lip!" I'm shouting again. I am so bad in these situations. This is why I couldn't be a Cobra. Not because I'm a woman but because in stressful situations, I turn into a panicked, high pitched teenage girl that doesn't know what to do.

"I bit my lip when you decided to try and whack me like Tyson fucking Fury, you lunatic!" Crow laughs as he comes closer again, letting me see the damage I'd done.

"It's already starting to bruise. Oh bloody hell, I'm sorry." I wince as I brush my fingers gently over the already purplish skin, knowing that not only must it hurt but that I've caused it.

"It's fine, I've had worse. I just wasn't expecting a decent punch to come from you," he tells me lightly with a smirk.

"Oh shut up and let me get some ice." I rush back into the house and get a bag of ice from the freezer before resting it on Crow's chin as he tilts his head back.

The garden is surrounded by high fencing and bushes meaning that no one can see in and with Dad at the Club getting ready for the meeting later, no one is around to witness what we're doing.

Crow's eyes are dark as I edge closer to him, our faces only inches apart. The blood on his lips has vanished, and as he looks at me, I feel the heat I've wondered about time and time again. His eyebrows crease together in wonder and as I find myself instinctually leaning closer to him, he puts his arm around my waist softly.

"How does it feel now?" I whisper quietly.

"It feels good." His voice is low, gentle. I can feel his breath on my face as he speaks.

"Close your eyes." I don't know where this bravery is coming from but he does as I demand. His eyelids bat shut.

I bring myself closer to his lips and place mine delicately on the already bruised mark on his face.

His skin was soft and warm, almost feather-like against my lips. The hand that rests around my waist pulls me in closer to him.

"Char." He breathes my name, igniting a fever within me. We have never spoken about how I feel, I have never questioned if he feels the same way. I am instantly warmed by the thought of Crow wanting this, *us,* as much as I do.

The bravery leaves me just as quickly as it had come, and it leaves me in a state of timid embarrassment for having kissed Crow. Even if it was just a peck on the side of his lip.

"Char, look at me." His voice is demanding, yet soft.

"Yeah, I don't think so. I'm sorry." I laugh awkwardly.

His hand reaches for my chin and lifts my face to look at his. I do so, sheepishly.

"What was that?" he asks, his face flat and patient.

"A kiss to make it all better?" I squeak out in question with a small laugh.

He doesn't say anything, but his brows crease as if he's never heard of anything so absurd before.

"Why?"

"Why do you think? I'm just gonna go inside," I tell him as I pull my face away from his hand and turn towards the house.

He grasps my wrist and yanks me back to him so that our bodies are flush up against one another.

I can feel the muscles of his chest on my breasts and feel the fire ignite within me once more.

"Do it again, but don't be sorry this time." His words hit me like a freight train, making my brows rise in shock. He wants me to do it again?

I look into his eyes, waiting for him to shake his head, to change his mind or laugh at me but he does none of that. Instead, his eyes bore into mine hungrily, waiting.

I look ahead and find that my eyes are the same height as his chest.

I spare one more glance at him to be sure he's not going to backtrack before placing numerous light kisses along the delicately soft skin on his chest, reaching my tiptoes as I ascend to patter kisses along his shoulders and neck before finally reaching his lips again.

All the while he stands there unmoving, staring at me in what I can only describe as awe and as he does, I feel more elated than I ever imagined possible.

Our lips touch. It's not soft or gentle, but rough and demanding. His hands nestle themselves within the waves of my hair as he pulls my head closer to his, destroying and maiming my lips with his own. His tongue darts out, eagerly swirling against mine as he uses his other hand to hold my body flush against his.

I can feel the heat of his body, his skin, the fire of the kiss we're sharing. It doesn't last long enough though. Within what feels like only a few moments, it's over and he's staring down at me once again. Only this time, I find myself unable to look away from his gaze.

Six

The Club is packed, same as yesterday. Same as every day. Crow and I are sitting in a booth towards the back with very few people within hearing distance.

The drive here took all of two minutes, meaning that no awkward silence really had a chance to happen. He's hardly said a word since the kiss aside from telling me that we needed to go to the club. He needed to be here for Dad's meeting and so did I.

I am supposed to be meeting the Laidens' President's son here this afternoon. I have already been dreading it, but adding the kiss between Crow and I into the complicated mess that is my life now intensifies the anxiety I feel about meeting a possible fiancé.

My dad has explained that there was a Cobras Only meeting first to discuss current affairs.

I would wait here, in the cafe as always when a meeting occurs; the only difference with today is that I have already planned to hopefully get close enough to listen in on the meeting. If no one will tell me what is going on then I will find out for myself.

Crow had rang ahead and ordered food. Alice had carried it

over, been tipped well, and has left us alone again. Even though I know Alice has a thing for Crow and I hate the very thought of it, I am no less than petrified to be left alone with him for the fear of having some awkward 'that shouldn't have happened' conversation which changes everything.

"Pass me the ketchup will you, Char." Crow interrupts my thoughts with the most mundane demand.

I hand him the ketchup and then go back to eating my chips.

"Why are you staring at me like that?" he asks.

"I wasn't staring at you!" I insist as I look away, realising that in order to look away, I must have indeed been staring at him without even realising it.

"Look at me," he demands.

"I really wish you'd stop telling me to look at you," I tell him as I dubiously look his way.

"And I really wish you'd get out of your head and look at me instead of overthinking," he tells me with a laugh. I can't help but smile at him; he's right and he knows it. He knows me well enough to know how my mind works.

He shifts closer to me in the booth so that we're only inches away from one another.

"I don't know what's going on with us right now but I don't want it to stop, but I also don't want you thinking things have to be weird because you can't keep your hands off me," he tells me with a wink.

"Oh, shut up and eat your stupid burger." I shove him and watch as he laughs before digging into his food again with a smile.

"What times the meeting?" I ask, watching the room as most of the high ranking Cobras begin filing out into the hall. Crow seems to notice this just as I do. He checks the time on his phone before wiping his lips with the napkin at his side.

"Now apparently," he grunts out. "Right, you stay here. Do

not go anywhere unless it's inside this club, alright?" I nod at him, which is apparently enough to appease him.

"I won't be long, alright?" He gets up, grabs his phone, and heads out towards the hallway, chatting to a few of the men as he does.

I purposefully wait twenty minutes before leaving the booth, knowing that there are always stragglers that are late to the meeting.

There are still men around everywhere though. It's not hard to figure out that my dad has most likely upped the guards around the club or more specifically around wherever I am. Which is fine. I'm not leaving the Club.

I walk up to the bar and find Alice on her phone.

"Hey, Alice, can you do me a favour?" I ask quietly.

She eyes my suspiciously with a small smile.

"What's your plan this time?" She giggles.

"I'm just going to go for a walk, I'm not leaving the Club but if anyone asks, I went to the toilet, OK?"

"Sure, just don't be too long. They'll notice," she tells me as she eyes the men around the outskirts of the building.

I nod in her direction before heading off into the hallway towards the meeting rooms. The hallway is empty, so I take the opportunity and walk quickly to the room I know sits adjacent to the meeting room. There's a kitchen just off the meeting room that has access through one of the bathrooms, so I follow through until I'm at the door to the kitchen.

It must be my lucky day. The kitchen door is ajar slightly, meaning that I can see and hear straight into the meeting room.

My dad is sat at the head of the table with Tin and Dove to his right, Crow to his left, and John beside Crow. The rest of the men are sat sporadically alongside the rectangular table.

"It's a million pounds, Matt. We've already stopped two men from getting in the Club and one at your place. It won't be long before they stop coming in ones and twos and bring a whole fucking gang of the fuckers," Dove tells my dad.

47

"So what are you thinking? How do we get the mark down?" he asks him, though I have no doubt he's asking anyone that has an answer.

They're talking about me. My mark. A million pounds. Is that to get me? Who would be paying that much money to get their hands on me? When and who did the Cobras stop? I hadn't seen or heard of anyone coming anywhere near me that weren't supposed to, though I suppose that was with thanks to my dad and the men he had around me. I suspected that he had more people following me than he told me, but this practically confirmed it.

"I don't know, that's the problem. We have too many enemies to know who's behind it, though I suspect The Dealers have something to do with it," Dove tells my dad as some of the other men nod their head at his words.

"I've asked the O'Banians to help us. I've been trying to merge with them for years and they've finally got back to me. I just need them to help us sooner rather than later." My dad sighs, rubbing his forehead before taking a sip of the whiskey in front of him.

I recognised the name that they were talking about. The O'Banians, but I had no idea why or where I had heard the name before.

"They'll be able to take the mark down, won't they? Nothing's happening to that little lady under my watch, I'll tell you that much. Shit, they might even know a way for us to get some evidence of Gray's disappearance too." It's Tin that's speaking now, hopeful in the mysterious O'Banians reach.

"I really hope so. I don't know where to start with even half of the shit we have going on, if I'm honest with you men." I don't think I have ever seen my dad looking so defeated and worried. So vulnerable.

He has already lost one child, the disappearance of another would be the end of him.

"Liam's back tomorrow, he might have a better idea of how

we can face this, yeah? That little lady is the best protected little shit there is, I promise you that much, Matt. And with the Laidens joining us, no one will get near." I smile up at Tins words, knowing that he's as close to family as what my real family are, that he would do anything he could to help both me and my dad, even if it means handing me over to the Laidens in order to keep me safe.

"There's one more thing. Elio's got something on Gray, but I wanted him to wait until we were all together. What is it?" my dad asks, his eyes on Elio at the opposite end of the table to my dad.

Shit.

As I look up to see what else is happening, it's at that exact moment that Tin looks towards the kitchen door that I'm perched behind. His eyes catch mine before I get chance to leave. My eyes shoot wide with panic as he whispers something to my dad who nods in his direction, not looking towards me. Tin stands and heads straight towards the kitchen and as he does, I look to Crow, who I find is looking straight at me as well.

Fuck, fuck, fuck

I mentally curse myself for being the world's worst spy and begin to scamper off before Tin gets to me, but he's too fast and I'm apparently way too slow. I reach the hallway through the bathroom at the exact moment he enters the hallway from the meeting rooms entrance.

He looks from me to the doorway I've just come out of.

"What are you doing?" he asks sternly.

"Going to the toilet?" I tell him hesitantly, more a question than a fact, knowing that there's no way out of this unless a miracle comes to save me.

"What did you hear?" Oh shit.

"Nothing, I swear! I just heard voices and was curious but I didn't hear anything!" I tell him in a rushed whisper-shout so as not to gain any attention from anyone else. If Tin tells Dad I'm going to be in so much trouble.

Tin grins at me and shakes his head as he breaks out a rough guffaw of laughter.

"You're such a liar, you little sod." He laughs.

I smile up at him, knowing that if anything, I'm lucky it was him that caught me rather than any of the others. Although Crow saw me, too, that's not so great.

"Don't say a damn word and stop spying on us. For you own sake, stop spying, you're bloody awful at it," he says with a laugh before walking off back into the meeting.

Now there's just Crow to contend with. One down, one to go.

"What the hell was that, Char?" Crow asks as soon as he gets back to our booth.

"I'm sorry! I'm sorry, I just need to know what's going on and I know you can't tell me or won't tell me or whatever but I need to know, especially because no matter how much Dad doesn't want me to be involved, I already am." I spew out the words, unable to stop myself before I take inventory of what I've said.

"I know you can't tell me, I know it's not that you won't, I'm just frustrated always being kept in the dark when it's my life just as much as anyone else's that's being messed with," I tell him with a sigh.

Until Gray disappeared, I had always let my dad keep me away. He didn't have to try particularly hard because I just wasn't interested. I was young, naive, and more interested in my friends and my future career than the Club, but between Gray being gone and now, I'm as involved in the Club business as anyone else in the Dark Cobras is, whether they like it or not.

I don't want to be. I know there's danger because of it but I had that choice taken away from me the moment people started to dig and found out that my dad has kids. Not as though they had to do much digging and because he has a weakness – two, that meant that despite his best efforts, Gray and I had no choice but to be involved.

And now I've got a hit on my head and I have no idea how to save myself, let alone get to the bottom of saving Gray.

"I'm scared, Crow," I tell him quietly.

"I'll protect you, I swear to you, Charlie. I will keep you safe. No one is going to touch you. I'd do more than kill and murder, I'd fucking slaughter and torture - burn the world to ashes to be sure you're safe." His words whisper to my inner worry and paranoia, knowing that he truly will do anything to protect me, but that I don't want him in danger anymore than I want myself to be.

"What happened to that guy, the one in the cell the other day. What did my dad ask you to do that you could do this time but couldn't do before?" I ask curiously.

I haven't thought about it since it happened with everything else that was going on but there didn't seem to be any anxiety surrounding him afterwards, unlike the last time my dad had taken him down there to do his mysterious task.

Crow turns to look at me, his face stern, eyes cast low as he says, "Protect you."

Seven

My dad had insisted that I meet Victor, the Laidens' President's son, in one of the meeting rooms. The very same one Tin had just caught me in as it happened.

He felt that I wouldn't want a show for this particular meeting, which I couldn't disagree with. I'm not sure if everyone knows of the potential deal up for the offering, but either way I don't need it to be public knowledge if it isn't already.

"Are you sure you don't want me to come in?" Crow asks as we walk towards the room.

"It's fine, I promise. Go back and finish your food, I won't be long," I tell him with a smile that has far more confidence in it than what I currently do.

He laughs abruptly, shaking his head.

"I ain't going fucking anywhere, Char. I'm waiting outside the damn door," he tells me sternly.

I roll my eyes but am silently grateful knowing that he won't be far away. It can't be the most comfortable of situations for him to be in – standing outside the door while the girl you kissed only hours ago is inside talking about marriage with a stranger. This isn't a fun scenario for either of us.

I smile up at him timidly before pushing open the door and walking inside.

Victor is the only one in here. I was expecting my dad, or maybe Tin or Dove to be here. I didn't expect for it to only be us two.

He's a big guy, with no skin on show, but large enough of a stance even when seated to clearly see that he's filled out and most likely extremely capable of causing some damage.

He has light mousy brown hair and a relatively soft face. I was expecting a hard faced, intimidating presence and although his presence could certainly scare, I don't feel that's something he is purposefully trying to do.

"Charlie, I presume?" His voice is low and the smile accompanying his words much gentler than I assumed it would be.

I can definitely see that this man oozes charm and is the complete opposite of most biker men I know. He doesn't have the same air about him. He seems more like a well spoken lawyer than an MC President's son.

"That's me." I smile awkwardly as I take a seat opposite him.

He watches me for a moment before speaking, taking me in or so it seems.

"I know this is a little unusual but I assure you, I will not be forcing your hand if it isn't something you don't want as well. I just want to make that clear right away," he tells me earnestly.

"So you don't mind what happens either way?" I wonder aloud.

He shifts uncomfortably in his seat before loosening the collar around his neck.

"It's not that I don't mind. If I had my way, I'd very happily marry you. This is something both my father and I have wanted for a long time. For him, it's the merge he wants, for me, it's you I want." His brazen nature and words shock me. He doesn't even know me, how on earth could he know that he wants me?

"I'm not trying to be rude, but why exactly do you want me?"

"You're a stronger woman than what the men around you seem to realise. I've noticed that they don't allow you to do much or have a huge amount of say. I have watched you for long enough, allowing me to know enough to make the statement clear and true that I want you." I'm not particularly surprised at his admission of watching me. Given my current situation, one more person that doesn't want me either dead or sold watching me isn't necessarily a bad thing.

"OK. So, aside from me – what's in it for you? Or your dad?" I ask.

"That's simple. We have a lot of power in favourable areas and with particularly favourable people that are able to help us in our line of work and we simply wish to branch out, but we're not willing to do so without some form of guarantee that we won't be betrayed. The Cobras and the men within the Dark Cobras will not betray us if you are with us. Family first is all of our motto," he tells me with a nod of his head towards the door.

"Your family is waiting outside this very door for you as further proof that even if they disagree, they will not stand against us if you are with us."

I nod my head at him, knowing that he's right. No matter who agreed or otherwise, no one in the club would go against the Laidens while I was a part of them.

"This wouldn't be like a conventional marriage though, I want you to know that. I'm eighteen, I have plans for myself and my future, and I can't promise you that we will ever be as a normal married couple would be." My words make it sound like I'm accepting of it, of the idea of marrying this man that in all fairness to him has been nothing but honest and open with me since the moment I stepped in the room. If I'm being completely honest with myself, I don't hate the idea. I don't particularly like it, but if the safety of those around me is a certainty then I could see myself getting on board.

He has been more forthcoming about the information he has than most of the Cobras ever have been with me.

"I like someone, one of the Cobras. I'm not sure how this would work around that," I tell him quietly, feeling shy having admitted it but knowing that I couldn't rightfully go any further with this conversation without saying it.

He watches me intently, his eyes boring into my own as he slowly nods his head at my admission.

"I would like to think that one day, even if that day isn't for a long time, that we would be a normal married couple, but I understand if that doesn't happen and as I said before, I will never force it upon you."

"But how would this work? I mean, I just told you that I have feelings for someone else. I won't lie to you. I don't know what I want with them, but I know I can't be with them if I'm married." This is a me problem. It isn't his fault, nor his responsibility, to give me an answer or to find a solution to my question, but I ask anyway.

He looks towards the door thoughtfully, contemplating my words.

"Would you date me? Until a wedding is confirmed, date me and then see how you feel at the end of it? I'm not asking for a commitment to myself alone, I understand you'll be pursuing this other man as well, but it gives you an opportunity to know me while also being sure you want this."

"I can do that."

That's when another thought hits me.

"What about Gray and the other Clubs that want the Cobras gone? How can you help us there? You want to expand, that's fine, but what do we get?" This feels strangely like a business transaction as I request something for us in exchange for me.

I am disappointed in how easily I seem to be convinced that this is the right thing to do by his words. I like to think that I'm not usually the type of girl to believe and fall for everything I'm told, and yet the way Victor seems to hypnotise me each time he talks speaks volumes.

He's a good looking guy. Probably an inch taller than Crow, built a little smaller, but no less muscle seems to be covering his body.

"I'm glad you asked. I'm willing to deal with the Devils Dealers and The Enforcers before a wedding takes place and Gray afterwards. I feel he'll be the more difficult task but as a sign of goodwill and to show you our willingness to work together, we will solve the problem of the club wars before any further commitments are made." It is a good offer. A particularly generous one considering they are currently getting nothing in return and may still not if they prove incapable of doing what Victor is insisting that they can.

"OK. Deal with them and when it's done, I'll marry you so long as you promise to find Gray next," I tell him sternly as he nods at me.

"One more thing before we allow the others back in to explain the arrangement. Until either we are married or until the day upon which this agreement is deemed null and void, you are now under my protection. I have heard of your marking and I assure you that no hair on your head will be touched by you unwillingly." His words both terrify and thrill me. His voice is demanding, his presence overpowering, and as much as I don't want his protection over that of what I already have, I say nothing as he gets up and opens the door for the others to enter.

My dad and Crow file in first, eyeing up both myself and Victor as if to make sure that I was still in one piece.

"You're OK?" my dad asks quietly as Victor's father and VP walk in.

I nod at him and pull Crow towards me to take a seat beside me.

"I'll explain everything later, I promise," I whisper to him quickly, wishing that I had the chance to explain now without everyone else around.

"So what's the consensus then?" Victor's father, Demetri, asks.

"We've come to the decision that the marriage will take place but in exchange for that, we will deal with the problems they have with the Devil's Dealers and The Enforcers before the marriage. We will deal with the brother, Gray, afterwards," he tells his father, who nods solemnly at us all.

I have met his father before. He is so unlike his son in his demeanour – much harsher and more rugged. The complete opposite of his son who is sat in a suit with the Laidens' signage on the back and chest. His father sits, similarly to most bikers I know, with his legs spread apart and the leather jacket with the club cut surrounding it.

"I think that's fair. Don't you?" he asks my dad, who nods his head at him.

I can feel Crow watching me, his eyes boring into the side of my head as if in hope of a telepathic explanation. I wish I could give him one.

Eight

Come Sunday morning, the weekend has been spent decorating Liam's room with Crow, ready for his return tomorrow and arguing with Dad when Crow's not around about Dad's unwillingness to tell me the things that I need to know. There have been hushed conversations all weekend between my dad and the Cobras that have been visiting more frequently than normal. Something is going on but I have no clue what. As usual.

Dad pulled me aside to "talk shopping", telling Crow that he just needed to add something to the shopping list—which was a terrible excuse might I add. As if Crow wouldn't know what the hell we were talking about. As if my dad really didn't think I wouldn't just go and tell him. I think my dad assumed that if Crow wasn't around when we had these snippets of conversation that I would be more willing to do as I was told - to be obedient. He was wrong.

"You are not supposed to know. There is a reason for that, darlin', you understand that, don't you? We're here to protect you, you don't need to know so you can protect yourself. That's what we're here for." Now normally when my dad gives me this macho man shit, I just let him go for it because it's easier, to put it simply, but on Sunday morning, before my run, before my morning cuppa and quite frankly, before I had the patience for shit, I wasn't having it.

"No, you know what, Dad? I might be your little girl, but you were the one that taught me to protect myself, you were the one that told me I could do it just as well as any man, so no. Now that I want to know what I'm up against so that I can protect myself, which again, you taught me to do, you won't tell me a damn thing." I take a breath and glare at my father. Not as though I can stay angry at him for long, but he didn't need to know that right then.

He sighed, rubbing his hands over his face, and looked up at me.

"It's expected, Charlie, it's what's right. You shouldn't know or be involved in all of this. It's not me being difficult, we have to protect you, you know that. It's what I'm here for," he told me quietly.

"I will find out what's going on one way or another. I get that you want to protect me and that's great because I'd quite like protecting from some lunatic that thinks he can put me up for sale like some second hand walkie talkie, but I need to know what's going on so that I can protect myself too." I walked on upstairs and carried on painting with Crow as if my dad hadn't just been a giant ass.

And that was how my weekend went, filled with hushed conversations with my dad, and painting and decorating with Crow.

I had been honest with Crow about the conversation I had with Victor. I didn't want to hold back from him or keep anything from him, so I hadn't. I wasn't sure how we would fit into that scenario but I felt better on both ends, making Victor aware that I had something going on with Crow and Crow being aware of the potential marriage to Victor for the sake of the club and Gray.

So now comes Sunday evening, and as I look into the room

that we've spent the last forty-eight hours decorating, I debate shouting my dad up to have a look.

I haven't purposefully hidden it from him, but since we've been at logger heads all weekend, he's not been up here to see his best friend's new room.

"Dad! Come here!" I shout down the stairs, deciding against being childish and letting him see. Mainly because I am proud of how well it has turned out and no matter how frustrated I am with my dad, I know he is only doing what he thinks is best. I don't agree by any means but I also know that if I was a parent, I would probably do the same.

The grey theme works, but I've been careful not to pick out shades that are too dark or too similar so that the room still has some light even with the less than optimistic colour decorating it.

I hear my dad before I see him, heavily stomping up the stairs, hanging on to the rail attached to the wall making him look far older than he really is. At thirty-six, he is still seriously young. A lot of people start families at his age, and yet my dad has had a full life with a family, even if the members of said family have dwindled significantly in the last fourteen years.

Crow seems to shy away from my dad as he gets closer to us, dodging him as he walks our way.

"Since Liam's coming home tomorrow, we've redecorated as you know. Crow's pretty much done all the hard work and I've just told him what to do." I earn a chuckle from both my dad and Crow at this, and it dissipates some of the tension between everyone.

Crow won't say a word against my father, especially not in front of him but with him being my bodyguard and my best friend as well as a member of the Cobras and my dad as his President, I unintentionally and selfishly put him in the middle of it all.

"Why am I not surprised to hear you've been using your

bodyguard for manual labour, my darlin' Charlie?" my dad questions as he shakes his head in mock disapproval.

"Oh, shush up, and listen to me old m-"

"Old? I'll have you know I'm still in my prime, young lady!" my dad growls at me as I sigh and try to continue on.

"Do you want to see his new room or not, Dad?" I ask.

I open the oak door in front of me but keep the main light off since it's only just starting to get dark. That and the fact that I left the bedside lamp on as well as the floor standing lamp.

I enter first and look around again. The bed is on the left as you enter the room, with the bedside cabinet on the left of that, and a lamp and a picture frame with an old photo I found of Liam and Dad on top of it. There's a dresser straight ahead in front of the double window and more picture frames along the walls, next to the floating shelves I'd attached, just below the fifty-three-inch television. The grey rug matches everything else in the room, with the contrast of the white desk, grey and white bedding, and mismatched sized picture frames around the room.

Dad walks in and takes a stroll around before standing in front of the artwork that took me most of the day today.

He reaches his hand out to touch it, before I snap it away.

"It's still wet, Dad, don't touch it!" I tell him hastily.

"It's perfect." He looks at me then before turning again to look at the feature wall I had created.

I got my love of mountains, hiking, hills, and the outdoors from Liam, so I did my best to incorporate it into his room.

I painted grey mountains, with darker ones behind it onto the wall. Instead of the sun, I drew the moon, and filled it with light grey, almost translucent pictures of us all from my child-hood. Pictures of Dad, Liam, and some with me and Gray in too. The stars in the night sky were made from glow in the dark paint, and jewels that I had found in the pound store.

"This is incredible, he's going to love it, Char." My dad turns around to look at me again and grabs me in a monstrous hug before I have time to think about it any further. Before you know it, I've got my dad's strong arms wrapped around me "Thank you, Char," he whispers gruffly. You can hear the emotion in his voice, and I forget all about his scalding of me about the questions. I'm not sure if he's saying thank you for the room or for letting him hug me but either way I take it.

I pull back suddenly, "Oh wait, you haven't seen the best bit!" I squeal with excitement, and grab Crow's arm and pull him towards the mountains painted on the wall.

"It just looks like a nice painting, right, Dad? Nothing peculiar about it?" I question with a raise of my brow.

My dads eyebrows knit together as he shakes his head "Just a normal wall," he says carefully, and I can't help the smile that spreads across my face.

"Crow, if you'd do the honours," I say, bowing slightly and elongating my arms to show my dad the very normal wall once again.

Crow steps forwards and puts his hand up against the highest peak on the tallest mountain and then looking back at me and sighing in exasperation. He knew nothing would happen and yet I made him join the show anyway.

"Why are you smiling, Char?" my dad asks me as another laugh escape my lips and I skip merrily over to my dad, hold his hand and lead him towards the spot that Crow was just stood in.

"Put your hand on the top of the tallest mountain, Dad," I instruct him.

He looks at me in confusion, but doesn't hesitate other than that and does as I say before opening and closing his mouth a few times.

Crow and I made a small square hole in between the timbers of the wall. Only small, but large enough to conceal a few things within. Crow did the electric aspect of it all, I just came up with the idea but at the top of the mountain, where a small fake star lies, is a button behind the star that leads to the cubby hole opening.

After a few minutes of silence and my dad looking around the new space in awe, he comes back out to stare at me with what I can only describe as complete shock.

"Well, now I need one! What makes him so special?" my dads asks with a face of complete seriousness, making me laugh once again.

"Oh, you'll get one, Dad, you will." I sigh, taking his arm as we walk out of the room. I take Crow on my other arm, dragging him along with me.

Having two of my favourite men on my arms makes me happier than I'd like to admit. It's so simple and yet it makes me feel more complete than I have in such a long time.

I'm laying across the sofa in the lounge next to Crow, with Dad in his corner chair nearest to the television. I have my head on Crow's lap, watching *Hide*.

We're waiting for our food delivery to arrive, and *Hide* is my favourite thing to watch right now.

It's about fifteen people that go on the run, with FBI agents, law enforcement, and many others searching for them. The people on the run have three hundred pounds, the clothes on their back, and a backpack with the basics to camp and then they run. The person or people that last the full amount of time without being caught win. The winner gets a significant sum of money.

I spend the whole time either telling Dad and Crow how cool they are for coming up with the best ideas to stay hidden or shouting at the television when the Hunters are close by. Then you have my dad and Crow who think they're experts giving a running commentary on the show – why would they purposefully go home when that's the one place everyone would look for them? Why would you stay in one place for more than a day or two unless you know it's an underground, undetected area? It is constant with them two.

There's an abrupt knock on the door, and as I look up, I realise that Dad is already up and heading towards the door.

Within minutes, our food is plated and in our laps as we continue to watch the programme that had been paused while we got comfy again.

These are the types of nights that I love. Relaxed, without trouble, peaceful and content.

We do this at least once a week, which alongside the amount of crap I eat day in and day out probably explains why I never seem to lose weight. I'm not fat by any means, but I do have more meat on me than most of the girls at the club that I look at and find myself wondering what it would be like to have a body so perfectly sculpted and beautiful.

They are all slim. No more than a size eight at their biggest, aside from Alice who might be closer to a sixteen, but she's certainly not big. She has the most gorgeous curves.

I find myself curling into Crow a little more as I get lost in my thoughts but halt when I look down at how we're now sat.

I ponder for a moment at how my connection to Crow looks. We're both eating. Me sat on his lap with both of our plates of food on my lap as we continue watching television. No one ever says anything to us or about us in that way, but I realise that us holding hands when we're shopping or me sitting in his lap eating food, sharing a bed, and so much more of our friendship looks like that of a couple. I wonder if Crow recognises that as well? Even before our kiss, we have always been pretty physically connected.

As I watch him, I take in how breath-taking his eyes are, how soft the shape of his face is despite the harsh jawline he holds. No matter how serious or stern he looks, he has a softness to him that I suddenly notice I'm drawn to without ever recognising it before. I've thought about Crow and my attraction to him many times but it's only recently that I've begun to think about him as more because rather than just admiring his body, it's his caring and protective nature that draw me in.

We spend every day and nearly every night together.

I could definitely understand why people would assume we are together.

Crow must have noticed because he's now looking at me with eyebrows creased together, "What's the matter, Char?" he whispers, as not to disturb Dad.

I look at him a little more before answering. "Nothing. I'm just thinking," I tell him.

He doesn't say anymore and turns his head back to watch the show I've now lost all interest in, but with the one arm he has wrapped around me, he starts stroking my arm. The contact makes me shiver. He's always trying to reassure and comfort me.

Crow reaches for the blanket behind us and places it awkwardly with his one free arm around my shoulders and over my lap, careful not to get it in our food. He noticed that I'm cold and warmed me, he noticed when something was wrong and questioned then comforted me. Now that I think about it, he does it all the time.

Crow and I share a bed pretty much every night. Sometimes he sleeps on top of the duvet and sometimes under, and I've never thought any more of it. I'm surprised Dad doesn't, but I think he recognises our relationship and sees the truth in it or at least the truth in Crow, knowing that he would never harm me.

"What do you want me to put on Netflix?" Crow shouts towards the bathroom door. He's probably sat lounging on my bed in his boxers as usual, scrolling with the remote through our options for tonight.

I look at the clock on my phone. 11.23pm.

"I don't think I want to watch anything tonight. I think I'll just go to sleep," I tell him in a voice so small and meek I'm surprised he heard me.

"Oh," he says. "Alright then." I hear the televisions roar spinning down as he turns it off.

Crow immediately looks up in my direction as I leave the bathroom and I see him subtly look me up and down.

"Fluffies again tonight?" He laughs. He's referring to my obsession with fluffy pyjamas.

"Fluffies keep me warm, you big baboon," I tell him with a roll of my eyes.

I lie back in my bed, lay my head on the pillow, turn so that I'm facing Crow like I always am in bed, and pull the duvet up over my shivering body. Crow looks at me as he lays down on top of the duvet besides me and faces me.

"What's going on in that little head of yours?" Crow asks in whisper. His voice is rough, as if he's got a cough, although I know he doesn't.

"Nothing," I say. "You can get under the duvet if you want." I can feel the warmth that his body gives off as he climbs under the covers to join me.

"Are you going to tell me what's wrong now?" he asks. He's staring right at me, but being careful, being quiet, as if he's uncertain whether or not I'll bolt any second.

"Crow, will you cuddle me to sleep?" I answer his question with a question of my own. A brave question.

He turns onto his back and lays his arm across the top of my pillow. I slide over to him and lay my head on his chest, place my one hand between us and the other on his stomach.

He flinches. "Shit you're cold." He pulls me closer and starts rubbing my arm and my back. He feels so warm, so safe, so secure in his hold.

"There's a reason I needed your body heat under the blanket." I chuckle.

"Does it never bother you that you never get time for girls, Crow?" I wonder. I'm talking into his chest where my head is.

"I've got time for you, haven't I? And with all the mayhem you make, and all the chasing I do to keep up with you, I don't

66

think I'd be able to stay interested in anyone else." He laughs. His stroking on my arm and my back slows now.

"Do you want time for other girls though?"

"No, you're my girl in every way. Char, I don't need another girl in my life." I'm still unsure if I believe him but I tell him "ok" and close my eyes whilst listening to his heartbeat under my head. It's fast, faster than mine and so is his breathing. Do all men breathe faster than women? Do I just breathe slowly? Without realising, I match my breathing to his as I sleepily trickle my fingers along his chest.

Nine

Breakfast is served.

I am sat with Crow on my left and Tin on my right, with Dad and Dove sat opposite me. This is how breakfast happens most mornings.

This morning was my dad's last breakfast in charge of the Club and the Cobras, but also the day that he gets to pick up his lifelong best friend from prison after serving time for a crime very few around me seemed to know anything about. Or maybe they do know and they just won't tell me – not as though I have asked in years but them knowing and refusing to tell makes much more sense than them not knowing at all. I mentally shake myself for ever believing that they didn't know. How would they not? There would have been court dates, police interviews, and newspaper articles. Hell, I could probably find out myself if I really wanted to.

There is an aura of excitement at the table this morning as everyone picks from the buffet in front of them and places their food on the plates in front of them.

I had picked up a sausage, a slash of bacon, an egg, and a few hash browns. Crow has about triple if not quadruple what I have on my plate and will probably go back for seconds and possibly even thirds. The man eats like he's starved.

Dad, Dove, Tin, and Crow are chatting animatedly. The faces of the men around me are scattered with smiles and laughs. I join in when needed. I am nervous. For far too many reasons to count. I am nervous about seeing Liam.

I watch my dad as he chats with the others with ease. He seems more relaxed than normal.

I think maybe he is finally ready to hand over the reigns. He has enjoyed his time as President of the Cobras but I think he is happy enough to let Liam lead now. Even though he will still be Liam's second in command and be at all the meetings, the work load and pressure won't land on him as directly as it will on Liam.

I pick my book up with one hand and open it to begin reading whilst eating breakfast with the others. The chatter around me doesn't bother me as I delve deeper into the world of dark romance that captivates me in a way very few things in the real world do.

I had been obsessed with creating lists and reviews of everything I had read for the past few years, but since Gray's disappearance, the stress of the rival gangs, and now my for sale tag, I haven't given much thought to my future, apart from knowing that I want to get out as soon as I can. I just don't know how to make that happen yet. I can't leave until Gray is back or we have answers about him one way or another. That's why I have put university off until next year. It doesn't feel right moving on with my life while Gray's potentially hangs in the balance.

There's suddenly a high pitched intermittent ringing in the background that interrupts my thoughts and my reading. My head lifts, and I realise with a start that it's the house phone. It's Liam. He was going to ring with a time to be picked up, Dad had told me last night.

My dad smiles to the others and practically sprints to the phone to pick it up. He's impatient as he listens to the drone of the robot voice telling him that there's a call for him from Wrexham High Security Prison, from "Liam" and asks if my father wants to take the call. Press one if you'd like to take the call. Press two if this is a wrong number. Press three if you feel scared, afraid or threatened in any way. I could still recite the recording they sent out to everyone before you spoke to your family member or friend. I've heard it so many times from the times that I did speak to Liam on the phone that it is reserved in my memory now as another piece of pointless information.

My father, of course, doesn't let it get any further than that. He accepts the call.

"Liam, my man!" my dad shouts excitedly, moving his free hand around animatedly as if he's speaking to Liam for the first time in ten years rather than the thousandth. Well, I'm not sure how accurate that number is, but it's certainly not far off.

My dad's brows shoot up, his eyes widening in surprise at whatever it is Liam's telling him.

"Alright, I can do that, man. I'll see you in an hour bud!" my dad tells him and promptly hangs up the phone. That's got to have been the quickest conversation I've ever seen them have. They are normally talking and gossiping like a couple of middle aged meddling women for over an hour. An hour for which I'm rolling my eyes usually just listening to Dad's side of the conversation.

My dad spins round so quickly, I'm surprised he's not got whiplash, and tells us, "He wants me to pick him up alone so we can talk, and then we'll meet the four of you and the others at the Club. No club girls, just Alice and Ben. We'll be there at eleven. Got it?" We all nod. No questions asked.

"Fucking hell, let's get goin!" Tin says as he jumps from his chair and practically drags Dove, Crow, and I along with him.

I stop to turn back to Dad and watch as he nods at me and begins getting his things together.

"Tin, I need to get dressed," I pant out, tired from trying to resist the pressure he's using to pull me along like an excited puppy. He turns back to me with confusion written all over his face.

"He's seen you in pj's your whole life girl, come on." The "on" in that drags like he's an excited child, dragging their parents out of bed on Christmas morning.

"I'll meet you there soon guys, okay? I promise," I reassure him and begin heading up the stairs before anyone can stop me. Crow, of course, follows me in my haste, whereas Dove's already out the door before he gets the chance to mess my hair up anymore, and Tin sighs up at me before running from the front door with nothing but glee on his normally sullen and paling face.

And now I must decide what on earth I wear to spend the day with these mad men.

I'm at the Clubhouse chatting with Crow at one of the tables set out for the cafe.

The men around me are loud, excited and somewhat annoying in their boisterous nature, although I can't blame them. They haven't seen Liam in years and Crow, Alice, her younger sister Kira, and Ben, one of the newer recruits, haven't ever met him.

Crow's anxious energy is obvious. His hands fidgeting with one another, clasped together in front of him on the table, his eyes darting around the room as if waiting for a bomb to go off any second, and his lack of conversation is more than anything a sure sign that Crow is as nervous as I am, although for vastly different reasons.

"Stop stressing, Crow," I tell him as I reach for his hands to pull apart the fidgeting hands in front of us.

He looks up at me and with those soft brown eyes that usually hold the hardest of looks and I can feel myself softening under his gaze.

"Easy for you to say, you've known the man your whole life, Char. What if he doesn't want to keep us on?" He's asked me this so many times in the last few weeks. I get it. I do. New leadership is frightening and with so many of the new guys having nowhere else to go, it's a scary prospect that someone might tell them to leave.

"I won't let you leave alone, you know that. Come on, come out the back with me. These lot and their fidgeting are even making me nervous." I don't tell him that I'm nervous regardless of the drinking and hollering happening around me.

Crow slowly rises from his chair with a sigh, the squeak of the chair moving is barely noticeable in the atmosphere that surrounds us.

I don't want to be the first to see Liam, and I don't want him to see me before everyone else so I start walking to the back door of the club, knowing that Dad will bring him in through the front ready for everyone to hone in on him like he is prey, although the very thought of Liam being the prey in a roomful of animals is almost laughable.

"You know your arse is about as round as a couple of beach balls in those leggings right now, Char?" Crow asks me with a chuckle.

I'm suddenly mortified and turn around to look at him in astonishment.

Did he seriously just say that my arse looks like beach balls?! Beach balls!

"It's not a bad thing. Jeez, if looks could kill and all that," he says with a smirk on his face that I can't help but want to smile at.

I turn on my heel abruptly, shaking my head in mock disapproval. I begin to head outside but before I get chance, I find myself knocked over by what feels like a brick wall.

I flail and look around, grabbing onto thin air to catch myself from falling, but within a millisecond there are tree trunk arms wrapped around me, supporting me and stopping my collapse to the floor.

I look up and I swear to whoever's up there, my time of breathing in this world is done for.

It's Liam.

Of course it's Liam. Why wouldn't it be? Attempting to give myself a mental face palm hard enough that it'll knock me out doesn't seem to be helping the situation somehow.

My mind seems to be blank and what makes it so much worse is that it isn't just my mind. It's silent. No one is saying a word. My body feels like it's on fire and I realise with a start that it's because I'm still in Liam's arms. Well, shit!

I pull myself away from Liam, only to be pulled back in by him for the type of hug he's never given me before. The last time he hugged me, I was eight years old, about a quarter of the height of his six-feet-five builder's frame and also didn't feel awkward as a shit stood in his arms.

I allow myself to relax a little though and I realise that I'm not really doing any hugging, I am being hugged. His arms are locked around me, and I am just cocooned inside of his arms that seem to be unrelenting and unmoving.

I can hear him breathing next to my ear, but before I have chance to think any more of it, I hear his voice for the first time in years.

"You're so grown up, baby girl." It's only a whisper and yet his voice is deafening. Not loud, or obnoxious, just so over-whelmingly manly and deep that every fibre inside of my now grown up body shivers at every syllable he says.

He always called me his baby girl. I used to love it and now I can't decide if I hate it for reminding me that he still thinks of me as that child he left ten years ago or love it because it's so comforting.

I pull myself away, and as Liam reluctantly lets go, I get a good look at him.

He's the same but so much more. As a child I never looked

73

at him as anything but family but having not seen him in years, I realise through a woman's eyes he's incredibly good looking.

His head's shaved, but it's growing back. You can see the dark hair growing in every direction. His eyes are sky blue, which is the most insane contrast to the rest of him, because he looks as bulky and bad now as he did all those years ago, if not more so.

I guess there's only so much to do in prison and working out is a pastime. Clearly a pastime he took up going by the sight of Liam.

He's watching me expectantly and it's then that I know I've said nothing to him yet.

What do I say? My god, it's like it's the first time I've ever met him.

I'm frozen. My body isn't moving, my mind seems incapable of thought, and both Crow and Liam are waiting for something. Something from me.

Liam's eyes soften.

"I'm sorry, it seems crazy seeing you," I manage out, my voice and words feeling so small.

Liam frowns, his eyebrows coming together but the confusion I see on his face is gone in an instant. He brings his arms back around me in a heartbeat and I breathe, letting my body droop into his. This time, my arms wrap around him too.

I open my eyes to find that my dad has walked in behind Liam. His eyes are gentle, his face etched with concern.

I'm in my room, sat on my bed reading, using the light of my fairy lights above me when I hear Dad and Liam come through the door. Probably drunk or merry at the very least.

Within minutes, I can hear my dad snoring downstairs. He's probably fallen asleep on the sofa. Dad can drink and drink and drink, but the moment he finds somewhere comfortable, his eyes close and he's dead to the world.

I hear footsteps plodding steadily up the stairs. Liam. The house is large enough to have privacy but not so large that you can't hear everything going on within it. Such as the steps that have stopped outside of my bedroom door.

Two soft knocks on my door stop my thoughts.

"Come in," I say.

I pull the covers over me, covering the vest top I have on. It's just typical that someone wants to come into my room the one night I don't have my fluffies on to cover me up.

My lights aren't on, only the fairy lights above me, which allows me to see Liam as he enters. It's still dark, but the small light that is in the room illuminates him.

He's changed in so many ways and yet also not changed at all.

It could just be my adult perception of him that's changed, maybe it's not him at all, just the way I see him now in comparison to the way I saw him ten years ago.

He stops in the doorway. Uncertain. Probably just drunk and unable to see in the dark.

"Are you alright?" I wonder, shifting in the bed so that my legs are crossed beneath me, in case he decides to sit on the end of the bed.

He notices that I've made space for him and does just that. The bed shifts under his weight, though not so much that it makes any noise, although it does jolt me slightly.

"I'm a little drunk, my girl," he tells me, "but I wanted to talk to you."

"Is something wrong?" I wonder aloud.

"No, no," he rushes out, "nothing's wrong, we just didn't get to talk earlier." His accent seems stronger, certain letters being accentuated more. I suppose that's the drink too.

"I know, I don't know what came over me." I laugh nervously, finding myself shifting again, unsure of what to say.

Things never used to be awkward between us. I wonder if he feels awkward too. If maybe I'm so different from the child that he used to know that he doesn't know how to form a new relationship with me now that I'm not sat on his lap with him reading me a book.

"I read," I say, looking up at him now, holding up the book in my hands to show him "I think that's on you," I tell him. "Reading to me constantly as a kid has me now obsessed with reading.".

I notice a smile form on his lips, only a small one, but I notice it all the same.

"Your dad says you're a bookworm through and through."

I wait.

"Do you know why people read?" he asks me.

"To escape for a little while, to relax, to see a new world, a new perspective, a new life to live in for those few minutes that the words are in your head creating the perfect story," I tell him with a smile.

"What are you escaping?" he asks me.

I feel my brows furrowing. I wonder if Dad has told him about everything that has been going on here recently. I know he keeps him updated on most things but he probably didn't want to bog him down with everything else immediately so I decide to do the same.

"I'm not escaping anything," I lie. "Books just give me time to breathe."

He's looking directly at me. He looks unsure. Unbelieving. What does he think I need to run away from? What has Dad told him?

"Yeah, yeah you're right," he says, shaking his head as if doing so will help with clearing his thoughts.

"Are you sure you're okay?" I ask again. He seems so lost. I'm not sure that's the right word but it's the first one that comes to mind when I look at him. Lost.

"I'm fine, better than fine." He takes a deep breath, "I'm

home again," he says, with more conviction and certainty in his voice this time round.

"You should get to sleep," he tells me as he lifts himself from the bed and walks back the way he came.

I don't say anything.

"Breakfast on me in the morning," he tells me with a smile on his face this time.

I smile back.

"Hash browns t-" We both stop, and I find myself grinning, similarly to the one he holds on his face, as we catch ourselves both saying so at the same time.

He remembers.

"Goodnight, baby girl," is all I hear as I see the back of him leave as he closes the door behind himself.

Maybe I'm just too tired to think properly but I'm sure there was something wrong. Maybe he's just not adjusting well, or he's overwhelmed with the day he's had. It would be understandable.

Ten

Liam is true to his word, or at least I assume it is him.

I wake to the smell of bacon, and more importantly, hash browns.

I shower quickly, and throw on a plain black, long-sleeved dress, black tights, and a hoodie overtop after brushing the knots out of my semi-dried hair.

I sniff the air around me again, reminding myself of a bloodhound on a mission. The food still smells fresh, so before I have the chance to get distracted and take much longer, I launch out of my room and down the stairs.

There is a spread on the table of cereals, fruit, and fresh juices. I am watching the back of Liam as he is moving something in a pan on the hob, apparently still cooking up whatever he had planned. I can't have taken too long after all.

I realise that he hasn't noticed I'm here yet and find a smile spreading across my face.

I tiptoe over to Liam, suddenly grateful that I didn't put any shoes on after all and just as the music on the radio begins again, I jump and poke his sides.

I'm laughing at his surprised startle when he turns and glares at me in mock anger.

Still heaving from laughter, I look down at him still smiling. "Better than I used to be, hey?" I question as I jump away from him and move to turn the bacon on the stove so it doesn't burn.

The laughter's still bubbling within me as he sets up the table.

"I could have hurt you, Charlie," he says sternly.

I'm not looking at him, I'm flipping the eggs now, facing the window instead of the far too serious man behind me.

I spin, ready to apologise, and find him just inches from my face and feel my breath halt.

No. This feels weird.

I'm not a lover of people being in my space at the best of times, let alone after just waking up.

"I'm sorry. I didn't think," I tell him as I stare for far too long into the silence alongside his blue eyes. "I used to try and jump scare you all the time, I just thought- I don't know, I'm sorry."

"Your dad told me about your boyfriend." I know immediately who he's talking about. I mean, who else if not Crow? There is certainly no other guy in my life coming close to anyone being labelled my boyfriend, although I highly doubt that was the word Dad used to describe him. I also note a series of emotions that cross far too quickly across Liam's face when he called Crow my boyfriend. I don't think I'll correct him even though it's not true. Not yet at least.

Does that mean he doesn't know about the potential marriage in the works? I suppose he could be on about Victor, though I can't imagine Liam calling him my boyfriend. If Dad had in fact told him about it, the last thing he would assume was that.

"What about him?" I ask as I spin back around, tending to the food, sticking with the assumption that he's talking about Crow.

"You shouldn't be getting involved with him or the club."

He huffs, takes a deep breath that I can hear far too loudly, and continues calmly "It's not the right way, baby."

His use of the word baby freezes me for a moment too long before I flip back round, glaring at the man in front of me.

"I have just as much of a right to know what is going on. Why can't anyone get that into their heads?" I hiss out the last few words, cross at him for coming at me the first sober moment he can about my involvement with Club business.

If Crow was right with his suspicions and Liam starts changing things around here, especially with the new recruits, I'll be leaving right along with them.

"You aren't right for the club. You couldn't do what's needed to be involved. Are you a natural murderer?" he asks me lightly, softly, gently. So much so that it sounds like little more than a whisper.

What is wrong with him? First he asks about my boyfriend and then changes the subject to lecture me on the club, calls me baby in a way I'm not too sure sounded as innocent as it should, and then asks me if I'm a murderer.

I feel my blood boiling, my hands beginning to shake. Why on earth is he asking me about being a murderer? I know he's been locked up for years, I get that he's changed, I understand that things have altered and it's going to be hard for him to adjust but if he's insinuating that because I'm not some violent bully that can pass the Clubs tests that I don't have the right to know what's happening then he's more deluded than I ever imagined.

"Murderer? No. However my specialty is in finding out what I'm not supposed to." I stare him down, craning my head slightly to see into his eyes, but refusing to give up if he insists on being such an asshole.

His face is blank, impassive, unmoving; and no matter how much it boils my blood, I'd be blind to have to say it isn't attractive too. Not to me personally but I can understand why so many women fell for him when him and my dad were younger.

My dad and Tin often reminisce over the days when they were younger and had women falling at their feet – Liam included.

He laughs, and then he laughs again, moving back to give himself space from me, laughing so much, so hysterically now that he's bent over slapping his hand on his knee.

"And what exactly is so funny Liam?" If he's laughing at me, I'll be half tempted to use the punch I practised on Crow on him.

Not before breakfast though. Or not at all, let's face it, I'm not that brave or that violent.

He looks up at me, wiping the tears of laughter from his face.

"My god, girl, you'd make most men piss their damn pants with that look," he tells me with laughter and lightness in his voice.

I stare at him absurdly.

He doesn't say a word.

I roll my eyes at his silence and swiftly spin and plate up my breakfast, walk towards the kitchen door, leaving his on the stove, and turning it up to the maximum so that I can smell it burn.

Is that some joke to him? My involvement with the club , or rather lack of is not a joke to me.

Honestly, is there a reason we need men around? Can I find some deserted Island where men are forbidden? That would be great right about now.

I take my plate up to my room.

The wafts of burnt food are hitting me already.

I feel myself smiling smugly.

My breakfast tastes wonderful.

I have been desperately trying to avoid Liam since the terrible failure that breakfast was, but no matter where in the house I go, his booming laughter and far too loud phone calls seem to follow me everywhere I go.

I am currently sat out in the garden, reading once again. Well, mainly glaring at the asshole through the kitchen window, but reading too.

I'm sat on a swinging bench my dad made a few years ago, and I have Crow sat beside me on his phone making a new playlist.

We do this a lot.

Just sit in silence. We're comfortable around each other and I like that.

"Why are you glaring at him?" Crow asks me, pulling me from my thoughts.

"I just don't like him right now," I tell him, not in the mood to talk about Liam.

"You seemed to like him plenty yesterday," he says, obvious confusion threading through his words.

I find myself huffing, turning to Crow and glaring once again.

"He just annoys me," I tell him. "He's arrogant, a complete shitstick, and a frustration I do not need," I say with certainty.

Crow is watching me, his brows knitting together, the one side of his lips lifting up into a small smirk.

"I see," he says before returning to his phone.

"Where would you want to go?" I ask him. "If not here, where?" I've turned back to look at the book I'm doing a terrible job of reading, but I know he's listening.

"I don't know." He takes a moment.

"Probably somewhere kind of like this. Some place in the middle of nowhere." I find myself looking at him again, noting how similar we are.

"I think I'd find myself some land, far away from everyone else," I say. "I'll have a spare room for you when you're annoying me and I kick you out of bed though," I tell him with a smile.

I can't imagine anything worse than living in a city. The hustle and bustle, endless people, lights, chaos, and sirens.

Peace, serenity, and silence on land that I can call my own, with animals, would be my release. One day it will be. I'm going to find Gray, figure out how to calm the chaos around me, and then go to university, find myself a home and live peacefully. That's the plan.

"The spare room can be for when you annoy me," Crow tells me, putting his arm around my shoulder and pulling me closer.

"I am not annoying," I tell him with a laugh. "I'm just so perfect that no one else can stand it," I say, moving back into his embrace.

"So perfect indeed, Char," he says with a chuckle.

I find myself smiling at his words but am soon rudely interrupted by the very devil I've been trying to avoid.

"How long have you two been together then?" I hear Liam ask as he wanders towards us.

"Did Dad tell you we're together?" I ask as I watch Liam saunter towards us.

It was only a matter of days ago that Crow and I kissed for the first time, and here Liam is asking us how long we have been together. We haven't even talked about if this is a thing yet, and now I have to find an answer to him that doesn't make me seem too keen to Crow in case he doesn't want anything more than this but also an answer that doesn't make me sound like too much of an idiot.

"No, but I can tell. You don't stay here though, do you, boy?" he questions.

"Yes, he does," I tell him with a roll of my eyes and a sigh. What is this? An interrogation?

His jaw sets as he looks at me. He doesn't even acknowledge Crow. I stare right back. Again. This seems to be happening too regularly, and he's only been around for twenty-four hours.

These staring competitions are going to end up with me having my face stuck permanently in a scowl at this rate.

"I don't think he should," he tells me, still not looking in Crow's direction.

I feel Crow shifting uncomfortably, unsure of what to do with himself.

"Dad's fine with it," I tell him, ice lining my words. This man. He thinks he can just say whatever he wants, to whoever he wants, and get his damned way. Well, not here, not now, and certainly not with me.

What happened to him? I feel horrible even thinking it. Prison happened. I know he changed, but the shade he has been throwing my way since this morning is becoming too much when he seemed so happy to see me yesterday.

He doesn't respond. He comes to sit in the wooden chair opposite us. He's trying to intimidate. His arms crossed, legs ajar slightly, his glare alternating between me and Crow every second his eyes can roll around to it.

"I'll come back later," Crow says, pulling his arm from around me slowly.

I latch onto his arm with speed, agility, and a crack that makes it sound like I just slapped him.

"No," I say. I look at Crow. "Stay," I tell him.

"Look, I'll come back later, Char," he says. "I need to get some stuff done anyway." He's pulling his arm from my grasp. This time I let him go.

I know it's hard for him. He would stand up to anyone for me, I know that much, but I also know that he hardly knows Liam, has him as a new Pres, and can't put himself in a vulnerable position with him.

Crow's gone and yet Liam and I are still left staring at each other. More like glaring actually. The only passion shown is anger, frustration, and on his part happiness that he's intimidated my "boyfriend" away.

"Not sure he should be able to scare that easy if he's here," Liam says, "with you."

I do not respond.

I stare and stare some more.

Liam smirks, and it's the most frustrating thing I've seen since breakfast.

Eleven

Victor must have gotten my number from my dad. Or from his stalking ways, who knows, but either way he had text me Tuesday afternoon asking if I was free that evening to go for a walk with him.

I was initially shocked that he hadn't asked to go for food to some fancy restaurant or to a film. That seems to be the normal type of first date that people go on, but then I remembered two very important things. The first being that he was a MC President's son so his idea of a first date would be very different to most teenage boys I had known in school; and secondly that he had himself admitted to having me watched which meant that he probably knew I liked to be outside – hiking, walking, running – just about anything so long as I had fresh air around me.

I had asked Crow how he felt about it, not wanting to go without speaking to him about it first, even though I didn't have a huge amount of choice in the matter.

I didn't doubt that Victor would take no as a solid answer without question if I suddenly changed my mind but with Gray's life on the line and that of my father's men; my family, I couldn't very well turn him down and change the rules of the deal now. I mean, I could, but I wouldn't. It wouldn't be fair to Victor or to those around me that are relying on this deal going well.

I know that I could have just said screw it all and either marry him without getting to know him or just say no to it all, but both felt too hasty. I have to give him a chance. I hardly know him but from what I do know, although I don't see myself falling for him when I have Crow that is slowly but surely stealing my heart, I feel that Victor deserves a chance and so do I. If I do end up marrying him, I want to know him, really know him – even if the marriage never ends up being a conventional one.

Crow had been surprisingly easy going about it all so long as I promised to be honest with him throughout, which of course I had and intend to be, but now that he is walking me to the club to meet Victor, he seems more tense. Understandably so. Just before we enter the Club grounds, I halt and grab hold of his upper arm, feeling his bicep tense as I do.

"Crow, will you stop for a second?" I ask him, ready to beg. I can't lose him, not over this or over anything for that matter. I need him more than he could possibly know.

His jaw is set, his eyes dark and his face a mask, showing no emotion. This isn't Crow, and I can't even blame him.

"I'm sorry. I wish it didn't have to be like this," I tell him as I fasten my body to his in a hug I have no doubt we both need.

His arms wrap around me tightly as he sighs into my hair.

"You don't need to be sorry, Char. I get why you're doing it, I just wish you didn't have to," he tells me as he lifts my face and places a gentle kiss on my forehead.

I look up towards him and find his soft gaze burning into me. It's more than just physically being able to feel him, it's all of him. His presence, his safety, his constant reassurance that overwhelms and completes me. Being in Crow's arms makes me feel like the world could stop, the people could disappear, and it wouldn't even matter because he would somehow find a way to make it OK. The warmth of his breath, his arms, and his love surround me in ways I spent my childhood dreaming of and it's in that moment, the moment I can feel myself falling for the man that I know I shouldn't, that I hear an abrupt clearing of one's throat. An intentional cough that breaks up our faces veering for one another.

I startle and pull away, worried that it could be my dad catching us in a compromising situation. No matter how much he likes Crow, I don't doubt that he would be unhappy finding us seconds away from kissing. But when I turn to see the face the noise came from it seems even worse than my dad catching us.

Victor.

His face is blank, much like Crow's was only moments ago.

Crow tugs me closer to him, kissing the side of my head possessively, his eyes not straying from Victor's.

"You go on, Char, your dad will be picking you up here afterwards and I'll see you at home later," he tells me as he releases his hold on me.

My body shivers instantly, not only from the cold around me but from the immediate disappearance of his warmth around me.

I nod at him and walk to Victor, ready to apologise.

I open my mouth to speak, but he starts before I have the chance to fumble and say I'm sorry.

"No need. You did warn me. Let's get going." He nods to Crow before putting his hand on my lower back and guiding me away.

"I am sorry, I know I told you but it's not fair for me to parade it around in front of you."

He lifts the helmet off his bike and hands it to me, helping me fasten it below my chin before putting his on.

I realise now that he's still dressed impeccably. He's in a suit again. Does he not get it ruffled and dirty on his bike, I wonder.

"I haven't had a woman on the back of my bike before so

yank on my shirt if I'm going too fast," he tells me before lifting his leg over his bike and encouraging me to do the same.

I circle my arms around his large chest, feeling the muscles beneath his shirt rippling and moving under my touch.

I can feel his heart pounding against his ribcage, the rhythmic beats keeping up with my own.

Maybe he is as anxious as I was about this. Even if he does feel he wants me, if what he had said was true about not having had a woman on the back of his bike before he probably hasn't had any woman that he has been particularly close to either. I don't fool myself by assuming that he is a man that doesn't have one night stands and hook ups, I have no doubt he does, but perhaps he hasn't ever been serious with anyone and the idea of truly getting to know someone and dating someone is as foreign to him as it is to me. Or maybe I am completely wrong and over thinking as usual.

The bike engine roars to life, vibrating beneath us.

As Victor takes off and the landscape surrounding us begins to blur, I notice that his body starts to relax. His tense posture eases and my body seems to follow along. My rapidly beating heart slows and I let the wind blow away the worries that plague me for a while.

It isn't often I ride on the back of someone's bike. Dad didn't like or allow it, but I understand now why so many of the Cobras wives say they loved it. I feel more free than I have in a long time.

The time it takes to get to the lake beneath my favourite spot is only minutes, but those few minutes feel like mere seconds. I am not surprised in the slightest that Victor has brought me here. He had admitted the first time we met that he had been keeping tabs on me, so his knowing my whereabouts and my favourite places to go isn't a shock; however seeing him dismounting his bike, putting the helmets to one side, and walking towards the path I used regularly in a suit is not something I had anticipated.

"Did you really think walking up here in a suit was a good idea?" I ask, watching as he tries to hide a smile.

"You'll find that suits are my go to attire. Biker jackets, leathers, and slacks are not something you'll find me in often. Even when hiking," he tells me with a smile.

"Do you not wear The Laidens cut?" I wonder, knowing no other club members that don't show off their clubs symbols and signage at every chance they get.

"I may be one of them but I like to think that I'm my own man, capable of my own decisions. I don't need a cut to prove who I am and who I am loyal to." His clean shoes are getting muddy. I watch his face as it shrivels up in disgust as he notices the same moment that I do.

"We can go somewhere else If you want. So long as I'm outside, I don't mind where I am. You don't need to get muddy to get to know me," I tell him with a laugh as his face falls.

"I thought this was your favourite place?"

"It is," I admit, "but that doesn't mean we have to be here. Come on, we'll walk around the lake. On the pavement, save your shoes," I tell him with a wink as I turn on my heel and head back down the dirt track.

"I only came here because I thought you would like it," he tells me.

"I do like it. I love it here, but that doesn't mean that you have to pretend that you do too."

"I hate hiking, or even just walking out like this. I don't see the point in it."

I laugh at his abrupt nature, appreciating his honesty.

"So what do you like to do?" I ask as we follow the curving path around the silent lake.

He ponders my question for a moment, looking thoughtful as he gazes off into the distance.

"I don't have hobbies, or a huge amount of spare time, to be honest with you. I read before I sleep every night though, so I suppose that would be something I enjoy."

"What do you read?" I can't imagine him reading romance and fantasy novels somehow, so I find myself surprised when he admits the types of books he enjoys.

"It's a little silly," he tells me as he watches me for a reaction. I make sure I keep my face straight, not wanting to make fun of him for whatever it is he finds so silly.

"I enjoy reading dystopian and apocalyptic books. I don't read any non-fiction, which my father has always found ridiculous. He didn't like me reading fantasy and fiction books growing up so I always hid them."

"I don't think that's silly at all. I mainly read romance and fantasy, but I like a few dystopian novels too."

"I'll make you a library when we have our own home. We can read all the fantasy books we like." The smile accompanying his words is like a child's that has just been told Christmas is coming early, and it breaks my heart because I'm not sure I can commit to living together, to building a life and having what he so obviously wants.

"Your face just fell. I'm sorry, I just.." The ease from his voice disappears.

"You don't need to be sorry, I just don't know how things are going to be just yet."

"Of course. My apologies." And I've ruined it.

"Under normal circumstances, I'm such a hopeless romantic, so in love with the idea of love that I would be planning a wedding and searching up kids names already and sighing at your charm, I just feel so tense at the moment with everything going on and with Crow that I just can't seem to let loose, you know?"

"I understand," he says solemnly.

"So you're in love with the idea of love? What does that mean exactly?" He chuckles.

His laugh is contagious, his smile so open and honest that I can't help but smile back. It's true what I said. I am a hopeless romantic and with the honesty he's given me, I have no doubt that if Crow weren't a factor, I would be able to easily forget the arrangement and very genuinely try.

"It means that I have spent years reading romance novels and have always been desperate to have someone love me the way the characters in my favourite stories love each other. I've always wanted that overwhelming, empowering, all consuming love that takes you by surprise." It makes me feel vulnerable admitting that, and I'm not completely sure why. Maybe because love isn't something that I talk about often with anyone aside from family, or maybe it's because Victor is practically a stranger, and yet I feel more comfortable than I imagined telling him whatever comes to mind.

"Is that how you and Crow feel about one another?"

"I don't really know. We haven't spoke about how we feel. I know how I feel and I know that I do love him, but up until not so long ago that was just as a friend. I know that the feelings I have snuck up on me slowly over time, which isn't really the love I always dreamed of, but he makes me feel cherished, safe and treasured, which is something I love in itself," I tell him honestly.

"I like the idea of having that. Is it wrong of me to crave that with you when you already have it?"

"It's not wrong of you to want it." I feel like I'm being so unfair to both him and Crow. Both know the situation but that doesn't change the fact that I feel like a fraud for intentionally getting to know Victor with the idea of marriage in our near future while also falling for Crow.

We've almost completed one lap around the lake and are nearing his bike again. There's no one around, the sky is beginning to darken around us. It feels much like my life at the moment. There's so much brightness to be seen, and yet every day something else seems to darken the atmosphere around me.

"Would you like to read with me tomorrow?"

"Read with you?" I ask, a little confused at his meaning.

"I feel that me coming to a place you like isn't really first date material, but perhaps you can come to mine and we can read together. It's not what I suppose most would consider a date and maybe it doesn't have to be, but I feel it's something we would both enjoy."

"Yeah, sure, that sounds nice," I tell him tentatively. It does. I don't think I've ever sat side by side with someone reading, but it sounds like the most peaceful thing in the world right now.

"Why don't we go now? It's still early." Both his gaze and his question is hopeful. He seems so vulnerable, so sweet that I can't do anything but nod and accept his offer.

Twelve

❦

His home isn't what I imagined. At all. I'm not sure exactly what I had in mind but it certainly wasn't this.

As Victor encourages me to follow his lead inside of the block of flats at the edge of town, I am surprised to see he doesn't live at The Laidens' Clubhouse or at least onsite or nearby, but that isn't what surprises me the most.

What truly shocks me is the inside of his home, in part because it is significantly more homely than I expected it to be.

It is small, quaint even, and yet it seems to ooze personality. There are drawings, paintings, and quotes on every wall I can see, with more bookshelves on the walls than I see in most libraries. His lounge is compact, with only one two seater sofa, a coffee table, and a television, but the main reason it is so compact is because of the books everywhere. Scattered all over the floor, on shelves, in bookcases, and his desk that sat at the edge of the room. The kitchen is open plan and behind the lounge, just a single line of cabinets and the necessities. There are even a few books in the kitchen on top of his microwave.

"Sorry, it's a bit of a mess. I don't usually have people round," Victor says as he shuffles around the room, picking up clothes that hang over the sofa and chairs before throwing them in what I assume is the bathroom. It isn't messy though. Cluttered perhaps, but not messy. The books that take up the majority of the space within the small room look unusually organised.

"This is literally my dream. You've got your whole flat as your own personal library." I laugh as I scoot around the room and find a few books I recognise and have read and others on my to be read list. Maybe we have more in common than I thought.

"Well, you can come here anytime you want to dream." He chuckles as he puts the kettle on and holds a teabag up to offer me a cuppa. His whole body seemed to relax the moment we walked in through his front door. Maybe the posh, well spoken Victor is a whole other persona separate to that of the one he truly is when comfortable in his own space.

"One sugar, please." I nod as I take a seat and continue gazing around at the mass amount of books surrounding me.

"I bet your dad has a heart attack every time he walks through the door of this place if he doesn't like you reading fiction," I joke, remembering what he had said earlier on about his dad and hiding his books when he was younger.

"He doesn't come here. No one does really. I've got one good friend that visits but apart from that, this is mine and mine alone," he tells me as he hands me the warm mug full of steaming tea.

"Thank you." I smile as I wrap my hands around the mug to warm my hands up.

"So what do you want to read?" He places his cup on the table before peering through his collection and picking out a few books and bringing them over to me.

He sits next to me on the sofa, though not too close. I'm not sure if it's because he's purposefully trying not to invade my space or because that's naturally what he would do with a visitor anyway. I find myself surprised at the butterflies that fill my fluttering stomach as he takes a seat so close to me.

"You'll have to tell me if you've already read them but this one is one I haven't read. I've been meaning to for a while but haven't got round to it yet. I have two of every book, so we can read together."

"Why do you have two of every book?" I ask as I pick up the one he's offering me and begin reading the blurb at the back.

"You'll think it's strange."

I look up to find him watching me intently, his gaze not faltering from my own. It feels as though he's inspecting me, unsure if he wants to reveal his truth or not.

"I sign my books. Every single one. I want to be a publisher, but I also want to write and every book I own, I sign, like a practice for when I eventually get to print and sign my own books," I tell him with the hope that he'll be willing to tell me his own book secret now that I've shared mine.

"That's strange."

"Hey! No making fun!" I exclaim with a laugh as I shove him playfully and feel my heart faltering at the breathtaking smile he gifts me with in return.

"Fine, fine, no judgment here," he says as he holds his hands up innocently.

"So what's your strange secret then? Why do you have two of every book?" I wonder.

"I lied before, when I said that I don't have any hobbies. I do. I beta and ARC read for new and upcoming authors. I do it in page. I got into the habit of annotating all of the books I read which means that there are scribbles, notes, and highlighted sections in all of my books but I like to have the original copy too so I get two of each. One I can annotate and one that's clear of any annotation."

"Loads of people do that, that's not that strange. I mean, it's got to cost you a bomb with the amount of books you have, but my secret is definitely more embarrassing than yours." I laugh.

I'm not sure if it's a conscious move or not, but he seems to shift closer to me. So close that our outer thighs are touching.

Only slightly, but I can feel the impending heat from the contact. Victor doesn't seem to notice though as he picks his book up and leans back comfortably.

We sit in a serene silence as we read side by side, catching each others eyes with little laughs or smirks as we get to similar pages and find funny sections in the same book we are reading. It feels like we are reading for no time at all but before I know it, an incessant buzzing starts.

"What's that?" I ask curiously as I flip across the next page.

"That, my dear girl, means it's time for me to take you back. Your dad wanted to pick you up from your clubhouse at ten and it's nine thirty now, so we'd best get going," he tells me as he collects the book from my hand, takes a bookmark, and places it in the pages I had got to.

As we make our way down to his bike outside of the building, I realise I was right earlier when I noticed his body relax when we got inside of his flat. The moment we reach the outside air, he seems to be on edge again. His posture more upright, his body tighter almost.

Being on the back of his bike with my hands around his waist as he speeds through the night seems even more of a comfort now than it did before. The vulnerability I often feel when on the back of a motorbike doesn't seem to peak once. I feel like I am flying, rushing through as the world passes us by on a machine that feels as alive as I do. I had experienced the thrill before, but I unexpectedly feel more joy and free than I have in a long time. As I grip onto Victor's shirt and feel him bringing his hand to squeeze mine, I can't stop my immediate smile from the contact he is initiating, no matter how small. His hands are warm compared to mine being ice cold from the weather and the rushing wind.

The clubhouse gates came into view only moments later, leaving the adrenaline and euphoria to drain from my body almost instantly.

I notice almost immediately that the jeep my dad ordered

Liam is outside in the parking lot, meaning that either Dad has borrowed it or Liam is nearby which, after the peace I've had with Victor, is the worst thing to think about. I used to adore Liam as a child but as an adult he seems to wind me up and think he can control me which does not bode well.

"Are you OK there?" Victor asks as I dismount from the bike, place the helmet back, and brush down my windswept locks with my fingers.

"Yeah. Yeah, that felt amazing." I laugh as I continue to brush myself down.

Victor chuckles at my admission before taking a step closer to me, leaving us only a foot or so apart.

As I look up into his eyes, I feel somewhat hypnotised by the attention that he gives me.

"I had a really lovely evening. If you're available, I would love to do it again in a few days." The statement isn't posed as a question, though I know it is one. I suspect he is more uncertain and more self conscious than I perhaps realised to begin with. He doesn't seem as confident as I anticipated that he would be. I had assumed that a man in his late twenties that practically ran a motorcycle club would be filled with cocky charm but Victor seems the complete opposite of anything I had ever envisioned.

"I'd really like that," I tell him with a small smile, feeling shy under his intense gaze.

"Let me walk you into the club. I know we're inside the gates, but I still don't like to leave you alone at night," he tells me as he places his hand on my lower back and leads me into the front doors of the club.

The heat and instant desire I feel from his touch startles me.

As we walk in, the eyes of the men and women around us seem to land on us, both watchful and wary.

To all of these people, both Club members and the women that escort and join them, Victor is a powerful and intimidating source of violence. To see the previous President's daughter with him is either a shock or a sign of probable things to come if they know anything about the arrangement that has been made.

While spending time with him, though it had only been a few hours, I note that I seem to have grown used to his size and his demeanour, so much so that the initial intimidation I felt from him has diminished completely.

"Thank you for walking me in," I smile shyly. "Do you want a drink before you go?" I ask him as I walk towards the bar, seeing an excited and smiley Alice most likely waiting for every piece of information I could give her.

"As much as I appreciate the offer, I should probably get back. We have a big day tomorrow. A meeting with the Devil's Dealers." His eyes seem to darken at the mere mention of the Dealers, a newfound look I haven't seen from him before. If he hadn't been so soft and sweet with me from the moment we first met, I could definitely understand why everyone was so awe struck and intimidated by him. He is a devastatingly handsome man that holds power and dominance in his every stride and word he speaks.

"OK, well thank you again for tonight, and thank you for what you're doing with the other clubs. I really do appreciate it, and I know everyone else does too."

"I'm more than happy to. I'll text you later if that's OK?" he asks as he lifts my hand and places a kiss on it before smirking at me slyly, most likely at my wide eyes showing both the shock and blush that seems to overwhelm my cheeks at his bashful and charming nature.

"OK," I squeak out as he smiles affectionately at me before turning to leave.

"Tell me everything!" Alice squeals in my ear as I watch Victor leave.

I turn to face her and laugh as she shakes my shoulders, squeaking with excitement awaiting any small piece of information she can get out of me.

"I feel so bloody bad, Alice, he's amazing," I gush, gladly taking the drink she hands to me.

"Why do you feel bad?" She laughs.

"Me and Crow have been getting closer," I tell her hesitantly, having suspected for a while that she likes him. "I'm sorry, I know you like him, Alice."

"What? No I don't!" She laughs, "Why on earth would you think that?" she wonders as her head rolls back with laughter.

"You're always blushing and giggly around him, I just thought.." I drift off, now unsure about my internal assumption.

"Have you ever watched me around any man under thirty? I'm awful around men, Char. If they're handsome or cute, I turn into a shy and blushing mess. That doesn't mean I like them," she tells me, still giggling.

"Oh, OK, well that definitely makes this less awkward than I thought it would be." I laugh.

"Where's your boyfriend?" I recognise the voice and roll my eyes instantly at the question being posed in my direction.

Liam.

I turn to face him, finding him right beside me.

"My not-yet-my-boyfriend is probably at home or working," I tell him sourly, wishing this conversation could end there but knowing without a doubt that he'll carry it on.

"So how was your fiancé?" I freeze at his words, the insensitivity behind them.

He's technically not necessarily wrong, but if he's been told about the arrangement then he should also surely be aware of the fact that the situation between myself and the two men that seem to be overtaking my life is a rather difficult and sensitive one.

"I'm not answering that."

"Oh come on, between your boyfriend and your fiancé, you've got to have some gossip to give me." His eyes seem hollow and empty, devoid of emotion, and I feel so bitter at his lack of care that I decide to leave.

"I'll text you later, Alice, I'm heading out," I tell her with a stiff smile as I take a step off the barstool I had taken place on and begin walking away. He may be the Pres but he is acting an awful lot like a cocky, nosy teenager instead and unlike everyone else, I am not a Cobra and will not give him the same bloody respect they do if he can't at least be decent to me.

"I'm giving you a lift home, baby, your dad's busy!" he shouts in my direction as he speeds up to catch up to me.

I hate when he calls me that.

Of course my dad left it up to him to give me a lift home.

"So back to your boyfriend then."

"He's not my boyfriend," I tell him as I steer my steps towards his jeep.

Thirteen

I'm sat in Liam's truck waiting for him and when he finally gets in, he doesn't go to start the engine. He sits there and stares at me strangely.

"What?" I ask. Knowing exactly what is bothering him.

"That kid's your boyfriend," he tells me. Not so sure of his words now as what he was only minutes ago.

I turn to look at him now, noting and reeling in his confusion.

"First of all, he's not a kid," I say before taking a breath that's loud enough to make me sound like a frustrated school teacher. "And secondly," I edge on, "he's not my boyfriend."

I watch as his face knits together, as if it possibly could anymore.

"You said he's your boyfriend."

"No, you said he was my boyfriend," I tell him with a smirk. "I didn't say anything of the sort. Crow's my best friend and maybe he will be more but right now we're just – in between," I explain, using my hands to express the said in between space.

"So, you don't have a boyfriend?" he questions. "At all?"

"Well, I mean, I wouldn't say not at all, but no I don't have an official boyfriend." I'm not sure if I would call it relief I can see on his face, but there's definitely something there that wasn't before, but it flashes by so quickly, it's hard to place. I remind myself that it's just because he looks at me like a daughter, or a sister, like family, that he's relieved. Though with the way he's been treating me since he's been home, it's been the complete opposite of care that he's shown.

"Huh," he grumbles, finally starting the engine. "Your dad's out tonight, won't be back until morning." He puts his left indicator on to take us onto the village. "Just you and me." Of course it is.

"And Crow," I tell him.

"Afraid not, he's going with your dad." I imagine that would be Liam's doing. Why did he even ask where he was before if he knew? Does he genuinely just enjoy winding me up?

"Where are they going?" I ask instead of asking what I really want to know.

"He says he has to go and meet some friends," he tells me. Not that my dad doesn't have friends because he does, but that is a lie. Dad doesn't go and meet some friends, all of his friends are Cobras and they either meet at the Club or come to our house. More lies. Why am I not surprised?

"Shit, that smells good!" I turn to find Liam walking into the kitchen, taking a seat opposite me. I place a plate in front of him, and head to the freezer in search of some ice cubes for my juice. My dad bought us a juice machine a few years ago, and I've used it daily since. It's the most incredible tasting thing ever. Even better with ice, though I normally forget to fill the trays up every night so it's not often I actually have the ice parts of that equation.

"Do you want a drink?" I ask.

"Juice will do, please," he says as he investigates the cottage pie.

"No beer?" I ask. It's not very often any of the Dark Cobras go long without a drink of alcohol in hand.

"You trying to say I'm some alcoholic?" he asks as I roll my eyes at his argumentative tone.

I pass him the juice and sit down to start. It does smell good.

"It's not often you used to go without a drink. I just assumed you'd want one now, too, especially after going so long without," I tell him honestly.

I dig in, and he soon follows suit.

"I'm changing, Charlie, is that so hard to believe?"

"What type of change exactly?" I wonder aloud. The only change I've noticed is that he seems to have it in for me since coming home.

"I'm making some changes to the Club and the Cobras to start with," he says, and with that I find myself frozen. This is exactly what Crow has been worried about.

"I'm cleaning my act up, taking charge like I should have back in the day," he tells me. "I want a family one day, a wife, a child or two, and I want the Cobras to be a safe place for them." What a contradiction. Dad always told me that Liam had a rough home life as a child and that's why he insisted on helping my dad raise me well and give me good experiences as well as keeping me away from the Club and the Cobras. Surely if he wanted a safe life for his future wife and child, he would want out. That's the safest way. Anyone related or attached to any Club member is in danger, no matter what.

We eat in silence for a little while.

Before I get too caught up in my own thoughts, I take my plate and his, expecting him to go back to wherever he came in from before he smelt the food, but I turn towards the fridge to find him sitting in the same position, no move to be made.

"I take it you're after dessert?" I ask. He used to take me nearly everyday to a cafe that specialises in desserts after tea as a child. It closed down a couple of years ago when the owners moved away.

"Well, if it's on offer, I'm certainly not turning it down." He sniffs the air like some dog before turning back to me.

"You get the chocolate, it's on the counter, and I'll get the fruit," I tell him, shaking my head at him.

We're soon enough sat back around the table with a bowl of melted chocolate in the middle and skewers filled with fruit and marshmallows by the side of it.

The melted chocolate and fruit seems to be the only thing we've spoke and not argued about so far since his return.

I take one before he has a chance and dip it into the chocolate heaven.

It. Tastes. Amazing.

"Your eyes are rolling, baby girl."

"Try it and you'll understand why," I tell him, ignoring his baby girl comment.

I'm too busy enjoying the treats on the skewer I'm holding to pay him much attention.

"I haven't had melted chocolate in years."

"Maybe if you didn't go get yourself caught with whatever you were doing, you'd have been enjoying it for ten years longer and telling me you're sick of it by now." My mouth starts to feel sticky from all the gooey sweetness, so I pick up the napkin next to my drink and wipe at my lips before taking a sip of juice to wash it down.

"You don't know why I was there?" he asks hesitantly, looking at me inquisitively now.

"Am I supposed to know?" I ask him.

He doesn't say a word.

"No one really tells me anything," I explain before getting my next skewer and dunking it into the chocolate again.

His hand is on my arm, stopping me from putting anything into my mouth. He pushes my arm to put the sweet stick onto my plate.

I find myself gazing curiously at him.

"Did your dad not tell you?" he asks.

"No." We're watching each other rather intently considering there's far nicer things we could be doing right now. Like eating chocolate covered strawberries and marshmallows.

"Are you going to tell me?" I ask him.

He comes out of his daze, shakes his head as if to get rid of the thoughts inside of his head.

"There were two men in our family, our club, not literal, biological family," he explains, "that I'd had my eye on a while. They'd been planning something and I needed to know what." I wait patiently, wondering where this is going. "So I go into their rooms when they're not around, look around and I find some notes." He stops, looks down.

"Plans to kidnap a child." He takes a deep breath, a breath so large it's as if it takes a physical toll on him to tell me.

"They'd planned it perfectly, and no one would have found them if they'd gone through with it," he says. "They were supposed to go through with it that night. So I found one of the men, tied him up, and went through his phone. They were going to kidnap the child for a ransom from her family. They had a list of kids they were going to take. It wasn't just the one. They were undercover, dealing with The Enforcers." He stops for a moment. His face is breaking, his arrogance gone. This is obviously difficult for him.

"There were messages between them on their phones about who would get to rape the child first, the things they'd do to her." I unintentionally gasp, covering my mouth with my spare hand to try and derail the shock spiralling through me. I'm not stupid, I know awful things happen in the world but to hear that it had nearly happened so close to home is terrible.

"The things they had planned for her I can't even repeat, I don't want to and I can't. They had a man on the inside, in prison at the time that was in on it too."

I watch him as he brings his face up to find mine.

"I killed the one man there and then. I was beyond angry, I was furious. I slaughtered him, ripped him limb from limb, Charlie. I couldn't stop myself even if I had wanted to. I had never, and to this day have still never, lost control like that before." Jesus. I can't even imagine what I'd do if I found information like that.

"I found the next man, but before I got there, I realised that I had to do it in public because I needed to go down to get this man on the inside. We have ties, connections, and many of them, but none of our men are behind bars," he says as he takes a deep breath again. "I found the second man in the square in town. I went up to him, paralysed him, ripped his cock off, and shot him in the head, and got sent down to do the same to the other one that was involved."

"I was supposed to be in there for eight years, even though I'd given the police all the evidence to prove why I'd done it. The judge commended me for my service to the child." He chuckles at that. "As if he was grateful. The extra years were for killing whilst inside."

"I'm so sorry." I don't know if he needs to say more, if there is more to his story, but I need him to know. I had judged him so harshly for so long, I can't help but feel awful.

I stand up, walk towards him, and crouch at his side.

"I always hated you for leaving," I say. "I mean I don't think I could ever actually hate you but it felt that way. I hated that you'd left me, that someone I loved so much had put the Club before me." I'm so ashamed of myself. Even if I didn't know, I should have known that he wouldn't get himself locked up for a reason that wasn't good. Wasn't needed.

He looks down at me, and I see something different now. I'm not sure if it's in his eyes, or in the reflection through his of my own, but the hate, the anger, the frustration. It's all gone.

"I sure hope you don't hate me, baby girl." He stops for a moment, though I know there's more.

"There was more than one child and even though I would

have done it for any child, it was you that fuelled the killing spree. You were on the list of names."

I freeze. I'm still on the floor next to Liam, staring up at him. Me. Whoever these men were, they were going to take me. Do horrible things to me. Possibly even kill me. I picture myself ten years ago, the innocence, the child that I was, and I want to cry in both anger and frustration but also in gratitude for Liam. Knowing that he did that for me. He spent ten years in prison to protect me. I'm sure he would have done it no matter who the child was, but to know that it was me both breaks and wrenches apart my heart completely.

"I'm so sorry." My voice is soft, barely there. I feel both ashamed and so grateful that I'm not sure which way my mind is taking me.

Before I have chance to stop him, he's on the floor with me, pulling me into a hug. Caring for me even after I've taken ten years of his life away from him. Guilt is over-riding my senses even though I know rationally that it shouldn't be.

I feel his hand under my chin, lifting it up to look at him again, and it's only because of the guilt and shame I feel that I'm doing it, otherwise I'm not sure I'd be able to bear looking at the man in front of me. Not the asshole. This poor man that threw away so much of his life to protect me. I was hating him this morning and now I can't even comprehend what I feel. Something between adoration and overwhelming guilt.

"I'm so sorry you lost your life because of me," I tell him with a shaky breath, my words cracking.

"I haven't lost anything. You're safe, and I'd happily do it again," he says, "I needed it." He sounds so strong, so sure.

I'm not convinced by his words, but after so long suffering because of me, or what could have been, I remind myself that he doesn't need tears. He doesn't need some girl crying and slobbering all over him. He's the one that's suffered, not me. So why am I crying?

I wipe my face, my hands wet from the tears that managed to leak, no matter how much I hate crying.

"I need some fresh air," I declare, lifting myself from his embrace. "Wanna come?" I ask weakly.

"I'm pretty sure coming would get rid of a lot of tension right about now," he jokes, and besides myself I literally burst out into the stupidest, most abrupt laugh in a long time.

Did he just? He just made a sex joke. He actually did. My God.

"Where are you going?" he shouts as I walk outside.

"To hell most likely," I yell back towards him. "But for now, I'm going to go sit on the swing," I say with a grin, watching as he chuckles to himself.

"It looks nice out here at this time of night." We had been sat in silence for a while, both in our own heads. The stars have joined us, and it is at times like this that I'm more grateful than ever for the lack of street lights, so that we can truly see the stars.

"It's my favourite place to be," I tell him. "Second favourite next to my bed, and the lake," I explain with a smile. "Have you seen your room?" I ask, having completely forgotten about the transformation I'd completed in there for him through the haze of anger and frustration.

"Yeah, it's insane in there, baby girl! Have you seen it?" Have I seen it? I bloody did it!

I turn to him now, wondering why Dad wouldn't have told him.

"I designed and decorated it, Liam." I laugh. "Of course I've seen it".

"Are you being serious?" I laugh again at his lack of belief in my skills.

I nod at him, taking a breath in and blowing it back out, watching as the cold air turns it to what looks like smoke.

"Do you know what it means when you blow smoke at someone?" he wonders, obviously thinking the same as me about how it looks like smoke.

"That you're a rude bastard?" I ask.

He chuckles at me. "No, that you want to kiss them." He smirks at me, but this one, unlike the smile from earlier, is filled with his usual arrogance.

"No, it does not!" I hiss-whisper at him, remembering I can't shout since we're outside with neighbours that probably don't want to hear us at this hour, shoving him in my annoyance. I'm not really annoyed, though I won't tell him that if he can't already tell. He laughs again, regaining himself from my probably far too forceful push of him.

"What is it with you and your terrible jokes today?"

He chuckles heartily at my words, shaking his head from side to side lightly. "Ten years away from women, and I think I've forgotten how to act like a gentleman."

"I'm not so sure that's true. Apart from the terrible jokes, you're not doing so bad," I tell him.

I look towards him in question when he goes silent, wondering if I had started another argument. I hope not after we have finally cleared the air between us.

I'm not sure what I expected to find when I face him, but it isn't the hunger in his eyes as he looks at me. The strange sensation I've experienced a few times since his return resurfaces.

He is handsome, I can't deny it, but the type of handsome you would think of an older man to be. He isn't old by any means, but too old and too close to family for me to find him attractive; and yet the way he looks at me—not just now but in a few separate moments before this—makes me think that perhaps he doesn't think of me as family in the same way that I do him.

It both surprises and creeps me out to think that he is looking at me with desire. He feels like an uncle, and yet the look he is surveying my way makes me question what I am truly seeing. Surely it isn't what I think.

Ringing.

It turns out that it's my phone chiming with a text that puts the odd moment to an end.

I grab my phone and stand, wanting distance from Liam and his uncomfortable gaze.

"Things got a little confusing for you there, didn't they?" Confusing for me? Right. Of course this is being blamed on me.

I'm not confused. I'm creeped out.

I look at him, my eyebrows shot up, attitude I'm sure covering my face.

"Confusing for me?" I repeat. "And why would that be? What am I confused about?" The damn cheek on this man!

"I'm more of a man than that boyfriend of yours for su-"

"Don't even bother, that's bloody disgusting!" I exclaim, cutting him off before he has chance to say any more. I stand and walk away, heading back towards the house.

Just as I'm about to reach the kitchen door, he shouts over to me.

"Charlie!"

I begin to turn, though if he thinks I'm going back over there then he's as crazy as every man around me makes out he is.

"It got confusing for me too." He's quiet now, but it confirms what I had already known or at the very least, suspected. The desire I sensed oozing from him wasn't in my imagination; he really has changed and not for the better.

My mind can't fathom that both the man that saved and the man now looking at me with eyes filled with hunger are the same. How could he save me from that torture and abuse and yet look at me with the eyes of a man wanting more than he should?

I can't tell Dad how uncomfortable he makes me, but I also don't want to be around him. I feel uneasy and vulnerable and I hate that.

I check my phone. Midnight. I seriously need some sleep.

Just as I go to drift off , my phone vibrates with a call from Alice.

"Hey, everything OK?" I ask as I wrap myself up and get comfortable.

"Yeah, I was just wondering if you wanted to come over soon. Kira's missing movie nights with you," she says with a small laugh. I hear Kira, her sister, mumbling something in the background.

"I will soon. I feel like we've hardly seen each other lately," I tell her glumly, realising how terrible of a friend I've been.

We used to see each other daily but lately I feel like my mind has been overrun with problems, Gray's disappearance, and the unrelenting tension between Crow and I—and now, of course, the proposed marriage.

"Did you find anything out when you were doing your sneaking?"

"Nope, I got caught. If you ever need a spy, do not ask for my help. It will not end well." I laugh, listening as Alice and Kira begin bickering about something before she comes back to the phone.

"I don't think I'm ever having kids. I feel like Kira is enough to deal with for one lifetime." She sighs.

Alice and I talk for a while, her telling me the incessant gossip that she overhears at the Club and me informing her of the constant chaos that sits around me before we finally hang up and I very nearly pass out from exhaustion.

Fourteen

L iam and I have been avoiding each other for two days now. Well, I've been avoiding him so much that I don't actually know if he's avoiding me or not.

I've thought it over, wondering what would have happened if the phone hadn't gone off. I can't decide if he would have tried something, leading to me having to push him away and cause a whole new drama in my life or if he would have kept the desire to himself, though with his crude jokes, inappropriate glances, and possessive questions about my not-my-boyfriend boyfriend and potential fiancé, I can't help but suspect that he will at some point at least try something that I know I will be uncomfortable with.

He's best friends with my dad. I have never thought about Liam in that way.

I'm so screwed.

I need to be concentrating on Gray and yet between Liam being too much, Crow that I want to see more than ever while he's constantly busy, and a deepening connection forming with Victor, as well as my name having a bounty attached to it, our club being at war and everything else, I can not think clearly.

Crow's been here daily, as usual, though he seems to be

busy and disappearing for hours on end, meaning that I've not had any chance to talk to him privately about anything. I've spent the days in my room, doing very little. Reading, eating, watching Netflix, and wondering when Crow will come back. Anytime it's just Liam and I in the house, I've made sure to stay in my room with the door shut, not wanting to be near him for the fear of him making me feel so awkward and uncomfortable again while simultaneously blaming me for it.

At the start of this year, I was determined to figure out so many things. My five year plan. My way out of this town. Finding Gray. And one day finding my peace.

I want to break away from the life I'm living and move towards the life that I have always wanted.

I don't want a complicated, dramatic, chaotic life. I want peace, tranquillity, and a home that you walk into and instantly feel relaxed in.

My mind instantly moves to images of Victor's apartment and how cosy, wholesome, and homely I felt while in there.

All my mind seemed to be able to comprehend right now is boys. Men. The useless half of the human species. OK, maybe not useless. They aren't useless, really. I just don't have the mental capacity to cope with anything other than the immediate troubles right now – finding Gray and getting myself out of trouble.

Crow had suggested a party next week and I had refused, but maybe letting my hair down and enjoying myself without overthinking every minute of every day was exactly what I need.

I've drank before but I'm not a huge fan. This party is at the clubhouse, which in one sense is great because it means I will be in a place that I am comfortable and I feel at home at. But it also means that everyone will be there, which I normally wouldn't mind, but the idea of being around both Liam and Crow doesn't appeal to me.

I suppose I could just have a few drinks and stay with Crow, and if I want to go home then I can. I can even stay at the club if need be, and I know I will be safe there.

Maybe I will go after all. I can dress up, make myself feel nice, and if I don't like it, I never have to go again. Right?

Crow has gone out to run some errands for Dad, so I have been left bored in the house alone.

I decide to venture downstairs and look for Dad since I have very little else to do and I know he is home. I still need to get answers out of him about the meeting and what the plan is about getting me off the market. I hate that I sound like a piece of meat being put up at the local market for sale. The thought makes me shiver.

Liam was supposed to be at the Club with meetings today. It is early, so I'm sure he will still be there.

Just as I turn around the corner into the kitchen, I hit something hard. I expect a wall that I've misjudged, but as I look up I realise that it's the very same creep I've been trying so hard to avoid.

I move to the left immediately in a hasty attempt to get out of his way before anything other than the very literal bump in occurs, but he of course goes to the left along with me, and then the right.

I stop. That's what you're meant to do when you're lost, isn't it? Stop exactly where you are and wait. Well, here I am, lost and waiting.

If any heros want to come and collect me now, that would be great please and thank you. Or not.

Liam doesn't go past me when given the chance though. No. He's looking me up and down, so slowly it burns.

I'm in my baggy shirt. Well, it's one of Crow's. He left it here a while ago, and I wear it all the time.

Liam still seems to be examining me. Actually, no, that's a complete lie. He's not examining me, it's my body he's looking up and down. The disgust that forms in my mind and convulsed through my body brings up an involuntary shiver.

I slap the underneath of his chin up so that he's looking directly at me.

"My face is here." I walk past him before giving him a chance to respond, knowing Dad won't be too far away, and since it's him I came out here looking for, I ignore the man behind me and carry on with my mission. Dad.

He's sat outside on the deck chairs. God knows why since it's January and cold. Great. Now I'm going to freeze.

I halt at the back door; my dad has got his back to me so is completely unaware of my presence.

I contemplate going back upstairs to change, but realise rather quickly that I am far too lazy to go upstairs, to get changed to come back to a spot that I'm already stood in.

I groan internally and spin, prepared to pick up Dad's coat from the coat-rack to at least keep the top half of me warm, but am once again met by what I now know isn't a wall, but a muscle filled man with no sense of direction.

I don't walk into him completely this time, I just come close. I internally roll my eyes at the frustration this man causes me any time I'm near him. Too close for comfort.

He brings his body closer.

No, no, no.

This is becoming very weird, and I am not liking it. I really need to talk to Crow. Even if I have to stay at the Clubhouse with him, it's better than being here and feeling disgustingly uncomfortable anytime Liam is near.

Such a large part of me feels guilty for thinking so poorly of him after his revelation yesterday and what he's given up to protect me but I also don't want to owe him something, that something being me, because he did that.

"Do you not think you should put some clothes on?" He's the Pres, technically in charge of my dad and just about everyone I care about, and yet he's acting like a menacing and ghoulish teenage boy.

"No one in this house should be attracted to me, so there

should be no problem with what I'm wearing." It's true. He practically raised me next to my dad for eight years of my life, there really shouldn't be any attraction there and yet with his incessant sex jokes, the 'confusion', and the constant bumping into one another, I'm sure there's something going on in his head that there shouldn't be.

Dad couldn't care less what I wear whilst in the house. Liam is supposed to look at me like a child, like the baby girl that he keeps referring to me as, the little girl that he used to play Barbies with, but, going by the tension between us now and the frustration on his face, I'm not entirely sure that's true.

"Are you bothered by me wearing so little, Liam?" I ask.

"Just put more clothes on." He spins abruptly and leaves.

I grab hold of a coat of my dad's, and head outside to join him. It's chill, the winter air blowing a bit, and I shiver slightly even with the coat. I sit beside him, then snuggle deeper into the seat, pulling my knees up to my chest and covering them with both the hanging material of Crow's shirt and the coat.

"I need the results back before then." My father's on the phone, talking to god knows who about god knows what. He's not facing me and obviously hasn't realised that I'm behind him yet.

I don't interfere, even as my insides shake a bit with fear.

I clear my throat beside him, and he acknowledges me for the first time, giving me a tight smile.

"I'm going. Two weeks, you hear me?" He doesn't wait for a response before hanging up.

Dad has only just figured out how to use phones that are anything less than twenty years old and now that he has, he seems to be on his twenty-four/seven.

He's only thirty-six, but that doesn't stop him from being incapable of understanding just about anything that is associated with modern technology.

"You alright, darlin'?" he asks, putting his phone down on

the table next to him and swapping its place in his hand with his mug of coffee.

He loves coffee, won't speak a single word to anyone before he's had a mug of coffee in the morning.

I can't stand the taste of coffee, but I love the smell of it. I think it's because I associate the smell with my dad, and it makes me feel safe and warm and secure.

"Yeah, I'm okay. I had something to ask you, actually, Dad," I tell him as I lift my knees up to my chest and pull the coat around myself even more. I should have gotten dressed. Well, more dressed. It's freezing out here. It looks beautiful with the way the leaves have fallen, and the sun that's sat in the sky, but it is misleading. It. Is. So. Cold.

His eyebrows lift, urging me on.

"You know the parties that Crow and all the other kids go to? There's one next week."

"That's not a question, Charlie," he says with a chuckle. I roll my eyes but laugh along with him.

"Well, I was wondering if you'd be ok with me going?"

"Course you can, darlin', you know you don't need to ask me. You are an adult now," he tells me, picking up his phone again. Probably playing some game on there. He's obsessed with Dig It, a game where you have to create tunnels to get a ball into a hole. So simple and yet he seems to find it so satisfying. The simple things, hey?

I know he's right. I don't need to ask him, but I always feel that I should. Whilst I'm living with him, it's only respectful to ask, no matter how old I am. It still astounds me that I really am an adult. That I'm in control of my life. A life I'm so lost and clueless in. I know what I want, and where I want to be, but getting there? That's where I seem to struggle. I have no idea how to get to the place I want to be.

"Ah, Charlie. We've all got check-ups with Doc that morning. The morning of the party. It's the Friday night, right?" The

Doctor. That's who he was talking too. What results is he so desperately after?

"You're not ill, are you?" I jump up, putting my palm to his forehead to see if he has a temperature.

I don't know how I will cope if Dad is ill. Seriously ill. It's my worst nightmare – losing him. I have no one else. No real other family. My mum's gone, Gray is nowhere to be found, meaning that my dad and Crow are all I have left.

I know that I will probably have a family of my own one day, and as much as I can't wait for that day, I don't want to lose my dad before it happens.

I'm not willing to lose my dad until I'm enough of an adult that I don't need him, and I somehow doubt will ever happen.

I'll always need my dad.

"No, Mother, I am not," he says with a chuckle as he knocks my hand away.

He always tells me that I mother him. Cooking him food, doing the washing, keeping the house clean.

I enjoy doing it. I hate mess. It stresses me out more than most people could imagine. A clean home means that I'm happy and Dad is less likely to trip over something and hurt himself. He still manages it mind; he's got two left feet like no one else I've ever met. It's not even that he's clumsy, he's just never paying enough attention to his surroundings when at home.

"Can I ask you about something else?" I question. He seems to be in a relatively good mood and is much more likely to not argue with me about my questioning without others around.

"Is it going to be a real question this time, darlin'?" He smiles.

"Yep, a real question this time." I laugh.

"Have you figured anything out about Gray or who or why someone put a mark on me? I know you don't want me to know but I need to know this," I tell him honestly.

He sighs, shaking his head before looking at me sadly.

"We haven't come much closer to anything with your brother. I wish we had but there's nothing, no matter which way we search. I'm not keeping that from you on purpose, we simply don't know anything," he says grimly.

"And as for you – Elio traced the Mark back to The Enforcers. The man you saw us with that day at The Club was the one that put you online, and if it was just them it would be fine but we suspect they're working with someone with more connections since no matter which angle we try and go through, we can't seem to take it down. They don't have that kind of grasp so we've asked another organisation to help us." The O'Banians. It must be them he's talking about.

"That guy, he said something to me before I left that day. With everything else going on, I forgot to mention it but he said 'He'll get you.' Who do you think he is?" I ask.

I haven't thought about the man's words since the day it happened, what with everything going on around me at the moment, but Dad's words remind me. He's not usually this open with me so while he is, I may as well at least try to get some answers out of him.

My dad's face ignites with fury the moment he takes in what I've told him.

"He said that? Why didn't you tell me before you left?" he questions. His voice has gone from quiet and soft to icy cold and nearing shouting.

"I didn't think, I'm sorry. I was panicking about Crow and I just wasn't sure if it was just his last ditch attempt to get free or if there was more to it." Lying to my dad never gets me anywhere so the truth it is.

"Let me make a call." And with that, he storms off, leaving me once again to myself.

Fifteen

I am happily watching Crow as he works out in the gym at
The Club. There is no one else in the gym at this time of
night, which means that Crow enjoys the time to release
any and all of his pent up energy even more. He gets on with
mostly everyone, even through the natural grit and grumpy attitude he shows to most people, but he also likes to have the gym
to himself and although I would usually leave him to it, Dad has
insisted that he doesn't want me home alone with the bounty
on me and since both he and Liam are busy tonight, I am with
Crow at the club.

I spend most nights with him anyway, though it isn't
usually here. I am more a middle aged mother than a teenager,
often tucked up in bed reading or watching Netflix by nine pm.

I can hear the music pounding from the main room. The
night is in full swing. There is music and mayhem most nights
but with tonight being Friday, the first night of the weekend, it
seems to give everyone even more reason to party. I had come in
through the back entrance to avoid the crowds of people. I
don't know how Alice sticks it, though I know part of it is just
out of necessity to provide for herself and her sister. They don't
have any parents around and with Alice being the eldest, she

feels that it is her responsibility to do what she can to keep them both in as good of a position as she can.

I place my book down, watching Crow as he lifts weight after weight and finding myself startlingly turned on by the sweat and grunts he is omitting. He only has a pair of jogging bottoms on, leaving his chest bare. The mirror in front of him allows me to see his face as it scrunches up, filling with tension each time he pushes his body further by lifting the weight in his hands once more. The muscles in his back constrict and release each time he moves. The sight of his strength and his powerful body leave my stomach in pieces.

"Like what you see?" I didn't realise he had been watching me as I watched him but as his eyes flit to my own, I shake my head at the smirk he has.

"I'd like it even more if you weren't working out and were over here instead," I flirt, though with my lack of experience, I'm not sure exactly what I plan to do if he does follow through with my plea and come to me.

"Well, if that's the case, I think I'm done for the night." He laughs as he places the weight down and saunters over in my direction.

"You wanna go back to yours?" he asks as he lifts my back-pack from the floor and sifts his arms through the straps.

"Can we stay here actually?" I ask weakly, knowing he will question why I want to stay in his room instead of my own. He knows I don't like staying here but the choice between being near Liam or hearing rowdy men all night had me willingly listening to said rowdy men.

"Why do you wanna stay here? I'm assuming it's not just to get a piece of this?" He asks, his voice filled with sarcasm and laughter as he bangs his chest like an ape.

"Nothing to do with any of... that!" I laugh out, playfully jabbing his side as we walk towards his room.

"So what is it?"

"If I tell you, you have to promise not to tell anyone, especially not my dad," I warn him quietly to be sure no one overhears.

"What is it, Charlie?" he whispers as he opens the door to his room and leads me inside.

I love Crow's room. It's so him. Predictable almost. Usually predictable can be bad but honestly, in all the chaos at the moment, predictability is perfect. I know I can rely on Crow, no matter what.

"Liam has been weird, it's hard to explain," I tell him.

"What type of weird?" His eyes darken at this as he takes a step menacingly closer, his hands wrapping around the tops of my arms.

"He's making sex jokes and looking me up and down, hinting that he wants, I don't know, something more. I feel like I'm probably just being dramatic, but he just makes me feel so uncomfortable, I hate it but I can't say anything to Dad. It would destroy him to know that the two people he cares about most don't like each other, and he's just got Liam back. I don't want to be the reason he begrudgingly sends him away." It feels good, better than I thought it would to let it all out.

"I knew he was fucking creepy from the minute he hugged you," Crow grinds out, shaking his head in disgust.

"He hasn't done anything, I just get this weird feeling, I don't like it. So can we stay here?"

"You can stay here whenever you want, Char, you know that," he says as he pulls me into his embrace, stroking my hair as he does. "But I do have a job tonight. A private job that I need to do. You can come if you want?" he asks with a playful smile as he pulls away from me.

"A private job? I thought you weren't allowed to do that."

I'm not one to be a stickler for the rules considering I break just about every rule I'm given – mostly unintentionally in a search for answers, but it's very unlike Crow to go against anything my father has said.

"It's about Gray. The garage that took his car from the

scene of the crash gave a report to the police and your dad, but when I encouraged them to be a little more honest, they said they'd call me back. They called me earlier to let me know that the mechanic that worked on it had some extra information for me. I'm going to see him tonight," he informs me as he begins suiting up.

I watch on in astonishment, my mind whirling with the possibility of a clue, the idea of getting one step closer to finding Gray. Crow is gearing up, filling his jacket with a pocket knife and gun, though I can't imagine he would need that to go and see some mechanic but with the things going on lately, I don't question it.

"When?" I ask eagerly, watching as he rummages around his room looking for things and filling up my backpack as he does.

"Now, if you're ready."

Crow takes my hand as I nod avidly in his direction. This could be monumental in finding out not only where Gray is but what happened to him. I've spent too long wondering, crying, and wishing that someone would find him and now here I am, with the predictable Crow who has done the most unpredictable thing – being the person that is bringing me closer to Gray.

As we leave the Club, everyone is too busy dancing, drinking, and cheering at God knows what to notice us, which in this instance isn't a bad thing. The music is loud, and the way people are carrying on, they wouldn't be aware of the Second Coming if it began right now. Perfect. We open the door on a wild burst of laughter, and as we step into the cold night air, the silence is an almost instantaneous thing. The noise from inside is muffled, and I breathe a sigh of relief that we slipped out undetected.

We clamber into Crow's truck silently and drive away from the Club without anyone asking any questions.

"The garage is a good twenty minutes away. I wanted to talk to you about something else though now that we have the chance," Crow tells me as he swings the wheel around, reversing out of the Club driveway.

"What is it?" I wonder, hoping he's not preparing to tell me bad news after bringing me so much hope from the mere mention of finding out more about Gray.

"What happened with Victor?" Oh. I should have seen this coming. I knew it would come and I knew that I would have to keep being as honest as I could be with Crow, but that doesn't change the fact that I feel full of shame for enjoying the time I spent with him.

"We went to his place and read, and I had fun," I tell him, not sure how much to divulge; it's not as though a huge amount more than that happened.

"How do you feel about him?" he asks, his tone clipped.

"He's actually really nice," I tell him honestly. "He loves to read like me so we literally just sat reading for hours. I do want to get to know him though. He does seem really sweet."

"I'm not sure sweet is the word anyone I know would use to describe him." Crow chuckles. "You just have a way of getting the untouchably formidable people to be soft teddy bears around you." He laughs as he shakes his head with amusement.

"You're not mad?" I ask timidly.

Even though I like to think I'm a relatively level headed person, I have no doubt in my mind that I would be jealous and somewhat possessive if I knew the person I was becoming closer with was getting to know someone else too.

Crow sighs and runs a hand through his hair before turning to look at me briefly.

"Nah, I'm not mad, Char. Obviously I'd much prefer if you were all mine, but I get it. Whatever is meant to be will be."

"I didn't take you as a believer in fate," I tease.

"Sometimes you gotta believe in something, girl, not much else to believe in round here." He smiles sadly.

We ride in silence the rest of the way. I spend the time contemplating how we can use whatever information we're given from the man we are going to see to help us find Gray. I really hope he knows something.

I had texted my dad earlier to say that I would be staying at the club with Crow and though he didn't usually mind and his response was a simple 'ok. Love you.', it was the text off Liam asking why I wouldn't be home that unsettled me.

"I don't think this guy's a danger, but you have got people on your tail so don't wander off, alright?" I nod to Crow, letting him know that I acknowledge and agree with his sentiment.

There was absolutely no chance I would be off adventuring the darkness without him. I like to think I was brave and strong like the characters I read about, but honestly, I would one hundred percent be the girl to run away and survive in a horror film rather than run towards the danger. No creepy basement hunting for me, thank you very much.

The man is stood in front of the bright lights of the garage sign above the entrance, waiting anxiously for us. He seems to be shaking, which could usually be blamed on the cold, but given it's currently warmer than normal through the winter in the UK, I suspect in this instance that the shaking is more nerves than the weather. His eyes are shifting and checking in every direction and his hands fidgeting together. His eyes light up when he sees Crow, who he quickly ushers inside the building. I follow quickly behind.

"Do you want a drink? I think I need a drink for this." The man is older than both Crow and I, probably in his mid to late forties, with a balding spot on the top of his head and a grey beard protruding from his chin. He looks innocent enough though, beside the alcohol and shaking.

I realise that I've spoken to him before. With my dad being a mechanic before joining the Cobras, he works on most of the bikes and cars the men within the Cobras have, but on the odd occasion that he doesn't have the time or the tools, he brings them here. I remember coming a few times with him and note that must be why I recognise the man.

"I'm fine. I just need you to tell me what you know," Crow tells him.

The man shakes his head as he tips back a single shot of what looks to be whiskey.

"You swear to me you can protect my family?" he demands, obviously scared about the safety of those he cares for.

"I already have people at your house now. They will be safe, I promise you that much," Crow assures him.

How has he got people looking out for this man's family? He said no one else knew about this and if that is the case, who can he ask to protect them? Surely he wouldn't lie and put this man's family at risk for information. I would do anything to find Gray, but leaving people vulnerable is not something Gray would want.

I need to ask him when we are out of here.

"Right, right, well, I had this guy come up to me the day the crash happened. Before it happened telling me that a car would be coming in later that day and that I needed to cover up and sign it off as an accidental crash – dangerous driving, speeding, you know the stuff I mean." He nods towards Crow before taking another shot.

"I said no, initially. I've been working in the industry for years, I didn't want to tarnish my reputation, but he had my daughters on his phone. They were walking home from school and he had someone following them. If I didn't do it.. he didn't tell me what he'd do but I dread to think." The man practically sobs as he holds his hand to his heart.

"I didn't have a choice, I couldn't let them take my girls. So when the car came in, I insisted that I work on it, checked it all over – it was the steering rods. They were left loose," he whispers to us in a rush.

"Who was it that asked you to put the clear reports in?" Crow asks.

"I don't know, that's the thing. He had a ski mask on, all I could see were his eyes. He was big but apart from that, there's nothing else I can tell you about him."

"I appreciate this, man. Thank you. You'll all be kept safe, I promise you," Crow tells him before taking my hand in his and walking back to the truck.

"Wait, there's something else." He's talking to me this time, looking directly at me.

"I think he knew. Gray. He knew something at least. I've worked on his car before, on his bikes when Matt couldn't, and we'd spoke about certain areas within the car that I wasn't to look in. I know who you all are, what you do. I don't care to but I know. I found this in one of the hidden spaces in the car." He hands me a small white, crisp envelope with my name on it.

It takes every ounce of strength and patience I have not to rip the envelope open there and then but I know that whatever is inside of it needs to be read another time. Not now.

Once we're safely inside the vehicle, knowing that we can no longer be overheard, Crow unleashes his thoughts.

"Your dad was working on his car the day before he went. He wouldn't have thought he did anything wrong, but maybe he left them loose and didn't realise. Maybe it was one of the Cobras covering it up for the sake of your dad's pride, his guilt if he knew it was his fault."

"He didn't. He wouldn't, not even by accident. Trust me when I tell you that someone did it but it wasn't my dad and it wasn't someone protecting my dad either. That doesn't explain where Gray would have gone either," I tell him sternly.

My dad and I have had our differences and disagreements but logically I know that he is good at what he does. He is a good mechanic. He has never made any major mistakes before. He double, triple checks everything he does, everything he works on and fixes. He wouldn't have made a mistake like that.

"Why would someone force that man to cover it up if they hadn't done it themselves or been behind it in some way?" I ask him, knowing that my logic in this area had to at least ease my dads burden and responsibility. It wasn't his mistake or nothing would need to be covered up.

"That's true. Whoever it is knows where Gray is," he concludes.

"Who's looking after that man's family, Crow? You can't just leave them with these people around," I tell him, the guilt gnawing away at me.

"They're protected. I wasn't lying, Char."

"By who?" I question.

"I don't agree with your dad on many things but I do in this – some things you don't need to know."

Sixteen

❧

I've been sat on Crow's bed with the envelope in my hands, staring at it for what feels like a lifetime. I feel both numb and tingly—one with dread, one from anticipation. I want to know, and yet I don't.

I was so desperate to tear it open when the man had handed it to me but now that I know that whatever is inside is potentially the last thing Gray intended for me to see, I'm petrified. What if it's a suicide note and we've got it all wrong about someone sabotaging his car? I know that he had been stressed over the last few months, but I had no idea if he had suffered with depression. Maybe he had. Perhaps I didn't pay as much attention to him as I thought. Would I have noticed the signs? Were there any?

What if it was a note to say that he was running away? Or maybe it was just a list of what he wanted to get me for Christmas.

I won't know until I open it.

As my fingers dance along the seal with trepidation, Crow comes barging out of the ensuite attached to his bedroom.

He has a towel around his waist, leaving the rest of his body bare and dripping with water from his shower. His hair is ruffled and messy, his face a soft mask of concern as he looks my way, and his body as tense and godly as every other time I see him.

"Do you want to open it on your own?" he asks tensely as he dries himself off and throws a t-shirt over his head, covering the sight of his bare chest and pulling me back to the moment. Gray's letter.

"No, I don't mind you being here, I'm just nervous. I don't know if I want to know what's inside," I tell him weakly.

He quickly goes back into the ensuite to pull some jogging bottoms on and then comes to sit next to me on the bed.

"I'm here for you, whatever you want to do."

His fingers lace through mine, filling me with the warmth and protection that Crow's mere presence brings.

"Whatever it says will help us in some way. That can't be a bad thing," he tells me quietly, and I know that he's right. Even if it's a mundane note that holds no real importance or relevance to the situation Gray found himself in, we'll know that we're not missing out on information, whereas if I don't open, we won't know if it does or does not hold information that could help us find him.

"You're right." I nod solemnly as I take my hand from his and open the envelope to find Gray's messy handwriting scrawled all over the page.

I'm hoping it's gonna be you reading this, Chars, and if someone else has opened it then fuck you, like seriously. Respect a girls privacy, will you?

Anyway, if you're reading this then I want you to know I'm going to look for mum. There's some shit going on in the world that is so much more than you could even begin to realise and I need to start working it out. Check my room, you'll find some stuff in there on where I am.

Either I've said goodbye and gone willingly in which case you'll never see this and I'm writing for no reason, or they've got hold of me because they know I know.

Either way, I'll figure it out and come back and explain it all. Promise.

Love you, Chars!

Oh and for fuck sake—stay away from Liam when he gets out. Tell Crow I was right and have proof but don't do anything about it until I'm home. I'll come back, I swear.

As I finish reading the letter out loud, my mind whirls. He was going to find our mum? What did she have to do with any of this and who was he referring to having got hold of him? What did that even mean? Does that mean someone took him? I rationalise that he probably felt he couldn't delve into too much information in case the letter got into the wrong hands but a little more of an explanation would have been great.

And then there's Crow.

"What was he right about?" I demand, angry that he had kept something, anything about my brother away from me in this mess we're in.

But Crow already has his phone to his ear, saying that stupid code thing again.

"Down Viper Spring."

I can't hear what's being said on the other side of the phone call, but I'm certain it's the same set of words that were said to him in the car when I was with him, and I'm doubting more and more the accuracy and truth behind Crow's alleged connection to some tech guy that he claims this person to be.

"He was right about Liam. He left a note saying he had evidence but not to act yet."

Who is it he was talking to exactly and what on earth had Liam done to warrant both Crow and Gray knowing enough about him to want me to back away? I know and feel that he has been acting unusually with me, but I didn't assume there was something more than him being a bloody oddball.

"I trust him. Yep, I'm about to tell her now. Both. Down Viper Spring."

I wait anxiously as he hangs up and turns to face me, his eyes filled with hesitance and concern.

"Right, so there's a few things I need you to know and a few things you can't know. You're going to be mad at me, but I need you to trust me. You got it?" It sounds rehearsed, his words, as if he'd practised this very speech a thousand times.

Do I trust Crow? Yes. Even if he is keeping things from me? Yes. I don't like it but that doesn't change the fact that I do trust him entirely.

"OK. I want as much of the truth as you're able to give me, though, Crow. I'm so fed up of all of this," I tell him, feeling my heart clammer and my stomach give way. I feel defeated, as if I've lost a war I didn't even know I was fighting.

His eyes soften and his face falls, my words bringing out the pain in him. He knows how much I hate being lied to and kept away from things. He knows how much it hurts me to have the person I'm closest to in the world do that, and yet I can also see the determination in his steadfast nod as he takes a breath and begins unravelling the lies that have been told to me.

"Do you know why Liam went to prison?" Crow starts.

That much I do know.

"Yeah, he told me about me and the other kids that were going to be taken by the men he killed," I tell him confidently.

Crow lets out a dark and sarcastic huff as he shakes his head at me.

"Officially, yes. But truthfully - not quite. Gray had suspected for a long time that there was more to that story than Liam had told everyone so he told me and we did some digging. We had spoken to one person who had told us a story that we weren't sure was true. He caught a lead and went solo to find out more but disappeared before I ever got hold of him to ask what he found, to find out if the story we had been told was true. That letter is confirmation that it was," he tells me with a sigh as he runs his hand through his hair before pinning his eyes on me again.

"Liam killed those men, that is true, but the reasoning behind it isn't. He didn't kill them because they were going to take you or anyone else. He killed them to cover up the fact that *he* was working with them and was going to take you too."

I can practically hear my mind whizzing and spinning, trying to make sense of the words leaving Crow's mouth. I almost wish that I doubted him but I don't. Not one part of me questions what I am being told. I wholeheartedly believe it to be the truth and that guts me completely.

"What's the rest?" I ask as I continue to absorb the information I've been given, feeling so vulnerable and dirty at the mere thought of the man I shared so many hours and days with as a child being not only willing and capable but actively part of a scheme to take children from their homes and do God knows what with.

"The guy I just called. He's not who I told you he was." I roll my eyes as he says this, having guessed that only moments ago.

"If you ever need someone and I'm not around, you call Kenny on your phone and say Down Viper Swing and tell them who you are. They'll protect you," he tells me seriously as I bring my phone out and check the contacts, realising that Crow must have added the number at some point without me realising.

"Char, look at me." I bring my eyes up to his, my own the shapes of orbs in the reflection of his deepening gaze.

"Do you understand what I just said, Char?"

"Yes, yeah, I understand, but who is it? Who's the person you ring every time something happens?" I inquire, looking at Crow in a whole new light knowing for certain now that he's a part of something I have no idea about.

"That's the part I can't tell you. For your own safety. I don't ever plan on letting someone get a hold of you but if anyone ever did, the less you know, the better." He stands from his bed and lifts me to encourage me to do the same.

"We need to go to Gray's room now. I'll explain more later but for now, we need to see what we can find in there." I nod my head at him and watch as his gaze turns from serious and business-like to soft and nurturing.

He brings his arms around me and tucks me beneath him, sighing and rubbing his hand against my hair gently.

"What's happening, Crow? I feel like everything is falling apart." I nearly sob into his chest.

"All I want you to concentrate on right now is you and me, you understand that?" he says, his voice a husky whisper in my ear. He lifts my chin gently with his finger and places a gentle kiss on my forehead, followed by one on my cheek and another next to my lips.

Before I have time to overthink and change my mind, I reach my hands around the back of his neck and bring his head down to my own, smashing our lips together in an undeniably and earth shattering kiss.

This kiss feels like the sun is rising, the earth is melting, the floor beneath my feet is shaking. It feels like the very molecules that make up every atom of my insides is roaring to life in both the anguish and passion that is consuming me.

I let my mind forget the chaos, the pain, the despair and the worry as I worship him and everything he's willing to let me take.

I want all of it. All of him. All of everything we could be when we unite. His lips feel like a fire against my own, his tongue darting between our lips in a war to take control.

For the single soluble moment that the kiss takes, I allow him and the thoughts of him to take over my mind, my body, my whole entity. My hands ripple through his hair as he clings to my waist lifting me so that my legs wrap around his.

I can feel him against my core. His want, his need, his desire, all matching my own in the heated tendril of war that consumes me as our lips collide and my mind clears of anything but him.

135

The roaring in my mind is interrupted by the very literal roaring in the hallway.

Crow puts me down in a rush, pushing me towards the bathroom as the crashing and screams appear closer.

Those screams aren't drunken fights or brawls. The bellows, howls and yells sound as terrified as I feel. The sounds ricochet around me, causing me to tremble. I want to clamp my hands over my ears, but I also want to know what is going on. It sounds like we're being attacked. And if we are, then why? Who? A volley of gunshots ring out, and I cower behind Crow even as he reaches for his weapon.

The door crashes open as Victor runs in, a gun in each hand, his face filled with fury and relief when he sees me behind Crow.

"Get her out. Take her to mine. I'll hold them off," he yells at Crow as he runs back out the door and down the hall.

"What's happening?" I squeal out as Crow grabs my hand and begins running for the door and dragging me down the opposite side of the hallway in the direction Victor just ran.

"I don't know and I don't care to find out right now. We need to go. Come on." He rushes out as we run along the corridor to the empty staircase. As we run down, the screams and deafening roars of gunshots grow.

"Fuck, stop." Crow drags me back, pushing me up against a wall as I hear more shots ring out at the side of the hallway that lead to the bottom of the stairs we are currently occupying.

Crow edges his head around to check the way is clear before he pulls me along to the back entrance door and runs for his truck, all the while holding my hand with a gun in his other hand.

Within minutes we are on the road.

"What about Alice and my dad? We need to do something, Crow, we can't just leave them all there to fend for themselves," I rush out, worry and anxiety for them building to the surface now that we are no longer in danger ourselves.

"We aren't going back. The chances are high that whoever it is wants you, not anyone else. I am not taking you back to a place where you are the one that's wanted. Between The Cobras and The Laidens, they'll be fine, I promise." His words do nothing to ease the dread that fills me; if anything, they just amplify the worry knowing that those ruthless enough to go after a woman for a bounty pay check will also be ruthless enough to hurt anyone they need to.

I pull my phone from my pocket and dial Alice's number, knowing that she above anyone else I care for is the most vulnerable in that situation.

"Charlie! Where are you?" Alice's voice fills the midnight air around me, and I breathe a sigh of relief hearing her voice.

"I'm fine, where are you?" There is no noise in the background, no shouting or screaming, no shots, so I assume she is either hidden or has been taken somewhere safe.

"I'm at home. Edgar got me and drove me back the moment it all started. I was so scared, Charlie."

"Edgar? As in Edgar, The Devil's Dealers Edgar?" My tone shoots sky high, inquisitive and worried once more, knowing that she's in or was in the enemies' hands.

"Victor made a deal with them. I don't think everyone's exactly on friendly terms but they are willing to help. He's gone now, but he was decent enough when he was here," she tells me, her tone filled with positivity. Alice is such a preppy and happy person that you would never be able to guess at the troubles she holds within.

"OK, as long as he was fine with you and he's gone now, I don't care. Is Kira safe at home with you?" I ask.

"Yeah, she's in bed sleeping, thank god. Edgar said he's posting guards for the next few days while everyone's still on high alert in case of another attack. Do you know who it was?"

"I have no idea. Victor rushed in and told me and Crow to leave so we're on our way to his, but I haven't heard anything else. I'm gonna go, Alice, I need to try and get hold of my dad, but you stay safe and call me if you need me, OK?" She tells me to stay safe too and hangs up, once again leaving my mind reeling and curious about the Dealers' involvement with it all.

"Did you know that Victor managed to get The Dealers on side?" I ask Crow as I dial my dad's number and hold the phone to my ear.

"Yeah, he told me earlier."

"Victor told you earlier?" I ask, paranoia making me wonder when they started having contact with one another.

"Yep. You're our priority, Char, we figured that keeping in contact would help with that," he tells me as his jaw sets and his eyes scan the road and the mirrors of the car to check for anyone following us.

"And you know where he lives?"

"Like I said, we've been in contact."

I don't even have a right to be mad. I'm not with either one of them, not really, and even if I was, I don't have the right to know every person they speak to. It just makes me feel like every ounce of privacy I once had has been stripped from me. In my mind, whether it be true or not, they could be comparing notes for all I knew.

I internally shake myself for even thinking that way about either one of them. I don't know Victor as well as I know Crow, but I do feel that I know them both well enough to know that they won't do that. Neither of them seem maliciously inclined to hurt someone.

"I need to get hold of my dad," I tell Crow. I'm just venting, releasing something, anything out of my mind in an attempt to relieve myself of one more factor that's worrying me. Three times I've rang his number and he's not picked up.

I try Victor's number instead, remembering that if things were over, he would be there with my dad or would likely know where he was.

The agonising wait while listening to the frustratingly repetitive ringing on my phone drove me close to insanity, leaving my mind to contemplate every bad scenario it could come up with.

"Are you at mine?"

"Oh thank god, you're okay." I breathe a sigh of relief at the knowledge that one more person is uninjured or at least not harmed enough that he could answer the phone to worry about me when it is him that was running towards the line of fire the last time I saw him.

"Of course I am," he says, sounding confused, as if the idea of him being anything other than fine was ridiculous. I can't help but laugh at the abrupt tone of his voice.

"Good, I'm glad," I tell him truthfully. "Is my dad there? Is he OK too?" I can hear noise in the background, men talking, both in hushed whispers and menacing degrees of anger. I can't hear what they are saying, but the anger is what presents itself.

"Your dad is fine, he's walking through with some of the others to make sure no one is hiding and that everyone got out safely. Are you going to answer me?"

The relief at hearing that my dad is safe is felt throughout my body. The speeding rhythm of my heart beating decreases steadily, my breathing relaxing and my hands began to smooth from the constant shaking.

Alice is OK.

Victor is OK.

Dad is OK.

"Answer what?" I ask, distracted, having forgotten that he had asked me anything to begin with.

"Are you at mine? It's not safe yet, there is likely to be another attack, it's how they do things," he tells me in a very matter of fact way, as if this whole thing is nothing but an inconvenience rather than a near fatal attack.

"We're nearly there. Who was it that attacked?"

"I'll explain when I'm with you. Do not leave mine." And with that, his voice is gone and the phone call is cut short.

Seventeen

C row and I have very awkwardly sat in Victor's flat for nearly an hour now.

I've only been here once before and I'm not sure if Crow had been here at all, though given the fact he knew where it was suggests that perhaps he has. Even so, he seems as awkward and agitated sat in here as I am. It is one thing being in someone's home when they are there to tell you to make yourself comfortable, but to be without them makes me feel like an intruder.

"Have you thought anymore about the letter?" Crow asks me as he puts his phone down on the coffee table in front of us.

I sigh, defeated, uneasy with the conclusion I had come up with but glad for the distraction, even if it is a dire one.

"Whoever Gray was talking about having taken him is with Mum in some way. I don't know if they're a gang, a MC, the bloody mafia, I don't know but the letter made it sound like mum was a part of them somehow."

"What happened to her? You've never talked about it. Neither did Gray," he admits.

I hate talking about her or giving her time in my mind because she just isn't worth it but maybe explaining why will either help relieve the burden of holding her a secret or possibly help him connect some imaginary dots to give us another clue in the mystery of Gray.

"I hardly remember her. I think I remember her face, but I was so young when she left that I don't even know if what I remember is real or if it's just imaginary from seeing her face in pictures." I recall looking at pictures of the four of us – me, Gray, Mum, and Dad in pictures when I was little and wishing she would come back. I look just like her. The same dark, wavy and wildly messy hair. The same eyes, even the same facial structure. Looking back now I realise that I look nothing like my dad and everything like her.

"She left when I was four. She told Dad that she didn't want this anymore. The family life, the kids, the husband, and that she didn't want to be contacted again. Dad said she left in the middle of the night after putting us to bed. She didn't want to say goodbye, so she just left. Dad tried to find her a few times but didn't come up with anything. He said I cried for weeks, but I don't remember that either. I just know that whoever she is, or was is someone that I don't want to know if she could just leave her family behind like that." I take a deep breath in an attempt to collect myself and my fraying thoughts. She isn't worth the energy I used even thinking about her.

"I'm sorry, it must have been shit, Char," Crow says as he rubs his thumb over the top of my hand in an attempt to comfort me in the only way he knew how.

I look up at him and find his eyes filled with the same deep sadness I have no doubt are in mine.

"What about your family? You never talk about them either."

"My family is complicated, let's just put it that way," Crow says as he chuckles.

"Oh come on, you have to tell me more than that! I don't even know if you have any brothers or sisters! Tell me something. Anything," I insist.

141

"Alright, fine." His eyes look around the room as if trying to find something to encourage a memory to pop into his mind.

"OK, so I do have brothers. Two. One younger brother and one older. My little brother Zak is hilarious, I mean so smart that it's hilarious. Like he'll come out with all these random facts constantly. He knows everything about everything." He laughs as he seems to be imagining him. "My older brother, Coran, reminds me a lot of Victor actually. He's the business man of the family, very straight faced. He can be harsh but he gives a shit, like really gives a shit. If he cares about you, you're set for life kind of thing, you know? They drive me nuts but I'm lucky to have them," he concludes just as the door opens.

I jump up to my feet, filled with both anxiety and dread, unsure of who to expect.

"Answer your phone, your dad's worried sick." The words come out of Victor's mouth before he's even fully entered the flat, leaving me feeling guilty for having left my phone unattended in the midst of such a chaotic situation. I pull my phone from the pocket of my coat hanging on the chair behind me and notice the numerous missed calls. All off Dad and Victor.

The phone rings again, this time allowing me to answer immediately.

"Is Victor there?" my dad's gruff voice asks. There's mayhem and shouting in the background, though it sounds more the voices around him are filled with anger and frustration this time rather than fear and danger.

"Yeah, he just got back, Dad. Is everyone OK?"

"I need you to stay there for a few days while I sort everything out. Crow and Victor are staying with you. The house is too dangerous for you to be at and so is the club. Until I get this fucking crap sorted, you need to stay put, you understand me?" It's not a request but a demand, one I dislike but know not to argue with.

"Of course, I'll stay, but you have to keep me updated and make sure that Alice and Kira stay safe too."

"They're in good hands, Charlie. I'll call you tomorrow and let you know what's happening. I love you." And with those parting words, he hangs up and leaves me stranded with the two men that I can already tell don't want to be stuck in the same country together, let alone the same flat.

"You can have the bed, we'll sleep in here," Victor tells me as he takes off his suit jacket, leaving only the white crisp shirt underneath.

I look uncomfortably around the room, wondering where they plan to sleep exactly. It's not the largest of spaces.

"I'll sleep in bed with Char, we usually sleep together anyway." My eyes immediately bore into Crow's, taking in his words and the heated glare I feel radiating through the back of my head towards Crow from Victor. I can see the smallest hint of a smirk on Crow's face, confirming what I suspected - that he said that on purpose.

It isn't a lie, we do often sleep together, but not at all in the way that Crow is insinuating, and he damn well knows it.

"Virgin Mary over here is declaring that I'll sleep in the bed by myself, thank you both very much," I say in a huff, knowing that if this is how tense it feels after only a matter of minutes in the room together that this is not going to bode well for any of us.

"You're a virgin?" The shock is palpable on Victor's face as his brows crease together and the out of place confusion fills his tone.

"Yes, I'm a virgin, job done. Thanks for coming to my Ted talk. Can we get back to a conversation that doesn't revolve around my intact hymen now, please and thank you."

"Right," Victor says as he shifts uncomfortably while Crow sits with the same smirk still plastered on his face. "Food?" he asks as he lifts what looks to be a takeaway menu in our direction.

Eighteen

"Your dad's just texted me, I have to go," Crow says, filling the awkward silence as he hastily gets up to leave.

"I thought we all had to stay here?" I ask, outraged at the fact that he can so easily leave and yet I've been guilt tripped into staying here.

"You have to stay, but your dad wants me which means I need to go. I'll be back in a bit, princess," he says as he drops a kiss on my head before leaving.

Victor releases a sigh of what seems to be relief as Crow leaves, which makes me feel even more awful for taking over his space.

"I can ask my dad to let me stay somewhere else if you want, I don't want to be overstepping by being here."

Victor looks up at me, confusion covering his face.

"Why would you be overstepping?" he asks, seemingly genuinely unsure.

"You hardly know me and I've taken over your home and had Crow thrown in, too, who you know and like even less than me. That's kind of overstepping in my mind." I laugh awkwardly.

"I like having you here, and it's not that I don't like Crow. I just find it difficult. We're very similar even though we may not outwardly seem it, and it's just a conflict of interest with us both wanting you," he tells me earnestly.

We met through a proposed marriage deal and since I had been so honest with him about my feelings for Crow, I wasn't expecting him to feel much of anything for me other than friendship at most. Hearing him say he's interested in me, wanting me, makes my stomach do flips and my heart race and pound so loud I'm practically certain he can hear it.

"You don't need to say anything, I know that was me over-stepping." He chuckles as he rubs his hand along the back of his neck.

"It's not overstepping, I just don't know what I want, and I don't want to pretend otherwise and make this worse," I tell him honestly.

"I get that. Crow text me about the letter from Gray," he says, changing the subject. "I've got some men looking for him, hopefully it won't be long until he's back home with you."

"Thank you, I appreciate you trying to help." I do. He doesn't have to help me and yet he is, so willingly, expecting nothing in return.

"OK, this is too tense, I can't deal with this. Do you want to bake a cake?"

"A cake? You want to bake?" I blurt out with a laugh as I watch him walk into the kitchen and begin getting ingredients out of the cupboards.

"Yes. I hate tension, it drives me nuts, so we're going to bake a cake," he tells me firmly, a small smile highlighting his beautiful features.

"Sure, why not." I giggle as I stand beside him and watch as he weighs out just the right amount of butter and mixes it with the eggs.

"How about you bake and I watch? You seem to be a pro," I joke, watching on at the face of concentration he's

145

making as he weighs out the perfect amounts of each ingredient.

He stops what he's doing before looking at me in mock disapproval.

"Only if you tell me something interesting while I'm waiting. Something no one else knows." A bribe. I see. I can do that.

"A secret for a secret, I'm not trading any of mine without getting one back." I smile, watching as he contemplates my offer before nodding his head, encouraging me to continue.

"OK, change of plan, how about truth or dare?" he asks before I have chance to say anything, looking mischievously suspicious as he smiles at me knowingly.

"Fine, but I get to go first," I insist.

The cake mixture is ready to be placed in the tray, which he does just as delicately as everything else he's done thus far.

"OK, go for it. Ladies first, I can handle that," he tells me as he offers me the spoon with some cake mixture on. I take it eagerly while I ask him truth or dare.

"Dare," he says confidently as he takes the spoon back and places some more of the cake mixture onto it before handing it back to me.

"I dare you to strip and run outside in your boxers," I tell him seriously. I expect a fight. What I don't expect is for him to hand me the spoon back with more of the cake mixture on it and begin stripping in front of me immediately. No hesitation, though if I had a body like the one in front of me I'm not sure I'd be hesitating to show it off either.

And, boy oh boy, do I thank myself for daring him to strip. He is as delicious as the cake mixture I'm currently devouring. He's toned - everywhere. Like, literally everywhere. His neck and his shoulders are bulky, leading to more muscle beneath his crisp shirt. I should totally play truth or dare more often.

"Just a light jog, is it?" he asks as he walks towards the front door. I nod, distracted by the rippling muscles moving and contouring under his skin.

Within seconds, he's out the door. I rush to the window, intrigued to see if he'll actually go outside and find myself surprised that he does. Not only is he practically naked, letting his manhood swing free (or very nearly free), and what a sight that is might I add but it's also January. In the UK. I get cold with three layers, let alone none, but he seems completely unphased as he looks right up to the window with a confident glance in my direction before leisurely walking back inside.

"Truth or dare?" I hear shouted from the stairs before he saunters inside. He grabs his trousers and puts them back on before walking over to sit next to me on the sofa topless. I'm not complaining.

"Truth." There's no way I'm giving him a chance to give me pay back for that.

"Are you attracted to me?"

"Is that a joke?" I ask, eyeing him up.

"No, I'm being serious."

"Yes, I'm attracted to you. You're bloody gorgeous, I'm pretty sure it would be impossible not to be," I tell him honestly with a laugh.

"My turn. Truth or dare." I offer him the choice once more before he has chance to comment on my appraisal of him.

"Truth."

I eye him curiously, his eyes glinting with mischief as he inches closer to me. I can feel the heat rising within my body having him so close and yet not one part of me wants to move.

"Don't you have club business you need to be doing?" I ask, knowing it's not the typical *Truth or Dare* question, but genuinely curious since everyone else I know within the MC life tends to be constantly busy with one thing or another.

"Honestly, not really. I'm called if I'm needed, and the rest of the time I'm here or with one of the few friends I have."

"Who's that?" I ask, suddenly unsure of if I've ever seen him with anyone other than the Inner circle of The Laidens or Cobras.

"Ah, ah, my turn," he tells me with a wagging finger mockingly.

I roll my eyes before choosing dare.

"I dare you to kiss me."

I wait a moment, wondering if he's joking and about to change his mind, but his face doesn't move, his expression unfaltering. It feels like he's testing me.

I only have to twist slightly to be nose to nose with him. I can feel and hear his steady breathing on me as I place my hand lightly on his cheek. His eyes don't leave mine, his breathing halting, seemingly afraid to move in case I change my mind.

I bring my lips to his and feel his lips graze mine, his hand coming to the back of my head. Not forcefully but encouraging me to continue. And I do. The space between us explodes in a new found passion as I find myself lost in the mesmerising sensation of kissing him. His tongue darts across my lip, testing the waters, though it's hardly needed. My body seems to react before I even think about what I'm doing. I open up to him, my body instinctively moving closer, wanting to be *so* much closer. He pulls me onto his lap, his hands on my behind, massaging every part of my body that he feels like grazing.

The kiss feels hungry, like it's been forever in the making. My hands find their way to the back of his neck and head, pulling him into me further as my body grinds upon the large, hard manhood beneath my core.

"Stop, stop, stop," he insists as he sneers and pulls back leaving me breathlessly steering away, unable to keep my eyes off his lips. That was not what I expected, and yet all I can think about is wanting more. He hardly touched me and yet I can feel how wet I am from just kissing him.

"If you don't stop, I'm going to take you to bed and fuck you." That gathers my attention as I look into his eyes and see no humour within them. He's deadly serious, and not one part of me would say no in this moment.

"I'm sorry. I got carried away," I tell him, feeling stupid for being so wound up and willing when I already have too many complications and uncertainties in my life. I don't need to add more.

He laughs before etching his head lower so he can look into my eyes.

"Don't be sorry, I fucking loved it. I just don't have much control when it comes to you grinding on my dick apparently." He chuckles as my face lights up with what must be the most furious shade of red embarrassment.

"Come on, the cakes gotta be done by now. You can help me decorate it. Just stay a foot or two away from me or I'm likely to relinquish the self control I'm stringing onto right now and fuck you anyway." He smirks before lifting me gently from his lap, taking my hand, and leading me back into the kitchen.

Fuck. Things just got more complicated.

Nineteen

I slept on the bed alone last night. It was surprisingly comfortable and I didn't wake once - unsurprisingly. I love my sleep. I'm now sat in bed with Crow who carried a tray of breakfast in for me. Well, burnt toast and a glass of orange juice, but who am I to complain?

"It feels like you and Victor are purposefully ignoring each other," I tell him. He didn't come back until we were both in bed last night. Well, until I was in bed and Victor was sleeping on the sofa.

"We've spoke plenty. Besides, I can't help it. He said he got called in. That's not on me," Crow says with his hands raised in mock surrender.

"I know, it's just shit that you don't get on. I care about you both," I tell him.

"You do?" he asks hesitantly.

"I kissed Victor yesterday," I rush out, feeling the full weight of the guilt and shame hit me all at once. I had stayed up late last night, thinking and over thinking about what I had done so freely without even considering Crow until it was too late.

Crow doesn't say anything for a moment, his face doing the

job of words and giving away his frustration as his brows crease and his lips purse together.

"I'm sorry. I don't want to lie to you but before you say anything, I want you to know that it doesn't mean that I don't care about you too. That's the problem, I really, really do."

"He's exactly the right type of guy for you, and I hate that, but I also know that you're the right girl for me so stay honest with me and I can deal with it. You're my girl and you always will be, no matter what happens," he says as he pulls me under his arm and into an embrace. My face to his chest leaves me hearing the erratic beating of his heart as I hear him breathe steadily above me.

"How about we make today our day? At least until Mr Kiss My Girl gets back?" Crow asks with a low chuckle. It doesn't shock me one bit to hear him be so casual in his jealousy. I know he's a possessive person and yet when it comes to me, it seems that no matter what I do or say, his care for me is never swayed. Something I hate myself for. I wish I could give him all of me.

It feels like in the moments I'm with him, he's all I want; and yet the same applies when I'm around Victor. If this is the part that a mum is supposed to help you with, I seriously need to find a replacement mother to give me answers to this teenage girls' problems.

"Yeah, that sounds nice," I answer him with a small smile.

"We've got to stay in the flat, your dad's being pretty strict about keeping you in here until he's deemed it safe everywhere else for you, *but* we could have a pamper day? I got some of your face and make up stuff from your dad's when I was out. I know how much you love pamper days," he says as he nudges me lightly with a teasing grin.

"Only if you'll let me put a face mask on you too."

"Fine, sure," he says as he rolls his eyes in defeat, which is quickly followed by my smile of triumph.

I rummage through the bag he hands me and find two

matching face masks before opening it and applying it to Crow's face.

"Don't pretend you don't love this as much as I do," I tell him gleefully.

He rolls his eyes once more before shifting so that he's closer to me.

"I definitely do not love it, but I can deal with it if it brings that smile out of you."

I don't think I've ever realised just how lucky I am to have that. This. Him. Since the first day I met him, he's always been so willing to do any and every thing it takes to make me smile which is when I note that I'm not sure I do the same for him. Or at least never actively. I need to set a day aside just for him. A day when I do whatever he wants, to keep him happy and make him smile. The thought brings another smile out of me. The idea of him being happy makes me happy.

"Have you heard anymore from mystery man about the mark or Gray yet?" I ask, having put the problems to the back of my mind until now.

"Mystery man isn't that mysterious, I promise." He chuckles.

"Are you going to tell me who it is?"

"No, you know I can't," he says regretfully.

As much as I wish he would tell me the things I long to know, I know him well enough to know that whatever he's keeping from me, he's keeping from me for good reason. I hope. I wonder if Victor knows. They seem to have spoken more about things than I had originally assumed.

"Well, until you do, he's mystery man," I insist.

"I'll make sure to tell him that. But no, he's made it clear how much danger you're in which is why I'm easily siding with your dad but apart from that, he hasn't got much yet. For you or Gray."

"I don't feel scared. I did when we were attacked, but I don't know. I feel like maybe I should be but I'm not," I tell him honestly.

"That's probably a mix between the adrenaline constantly coursing through you and you having two hefty bodyguards," he jokes as he pulls at his hair that I accidentally tangled in the gooey face mask.

"Maybe."

"You know I won't let anything happen to you. I don't need to tell you that. You know I'd burn the fucking world down before letting anyone touch you, so you don't have any good reason to be scared. I don't want you to be," he tells me.

I smile slyly at him, appreciating his words but not being able to take him too seriously when his face is covered in green goo.

"It's this mask, isn't it? Fucking women." He shakes his head in distaste with a small smile playing at his lips.

"What do you think your dad would say if you told him we were together?"

I freeze at the question. Unexpected and completely off topic. Partly because it's not something I really considered but also because it shows how serious he is about wanting us to be. He's usually the joker and I know he wouldn't ask if it wasn't something he wanted.

"If it ends up being that way," he quickly adds on.

"I don't think it would be a shock." I laugh. "I mean, he knows we share the same bed, we're with each other practically every minute of the day when you're not busy, and we've always been pretty handsy," I say, for lack of a better word. "So I don't think he'd mind or be surprised."

Crow nods his head in what I assume is agreement but says nothing else as I finish plastering his face.

My phone beeps as I begin opening the second face mask.

"Can you check that for me a sec?" I ask Crow as I attempt to tear the stubborn packet open with my teeth.

"It's Alice. She says she needs you to call her."

"Oh shit, I haven't spoke to her for days!" I exclaim, feeling like a love sick idiot for having forgotten about one of my only friends. The last time I spoke to her, she had Edgar the Enemy in her flat. I smile at my minds own nickname for him before pressing the call button and handing Crow the packet in disdain, unable to open it myself.

"I need your thoughts." No greeting, no questions. Straight to the point. Well, okay then.

"Sure, what's up?" I laugh as Crow begins applying the same green goo on his face to mine.

"I think I like someone," she rushes out with no more of an explanation behind her words.

"OK, tell me who, why and how it happened right now please and thank you." I smile as I tell her.

"That's the part I don't want to tell you," she says hesitantly.

My face scrunches up in confusion. "Why?" I ask slowly, unsure where this is heading.

"It's Eggy. Edgar. I think I like him. A lot."

My mind doesn't seem to register half of what she's said. "Eggy? You nicknamed him Eggy? Of all the possible things in the world that you can call him, you call him Eggy?" I laugh as Crow attempts to cover up his laughter opposite me.

"Well, Kira did and it kind of stuck." She giggles.

"Wait, Kira called him Eggy to his face and he did what exactly?" I ask, unable to imagine the intensely criminal man Edgar being called Eggy by Alice's teenage little sister.

"He looked at her a bit confused and then just kind of nodded and went with it. It was pretty funny actually," she whispers.

"Why are you whispering?" I wonder.

"They're in the other room. She's doing his makeup."

"This just gets better and better. Wait, hold on, what happened to him being the bad dude? He's a baddy, like a bad baddy, Alice, not tiktok baddy but *actual* baddy," I inform her before realising that if he was letting a teenage girl do his makeup that he maybe wasn't *that* bad.

"Most of the stories about him are bullshit, he's actually really sweet," she tells me.

"I feel like I maybe need to re-meet him at this stage Alice because I feel like we're talking about completely different people here." I laugh, holding my negative thoughts back. If she trusts in his apparent sweetness, then who am I to deter her?

Maybe I'll just ask Crow to get Mystery Man to do some checks, just to be sure. Alice is unbelievably pure in a world that doesn't deserve her kindness. I can imagine her forgiving anyone for anything but this is taking it to the extremes. Even for her.

"He's hardly left our sides since he dropped us off the other night. He's honestly been so lovely, Char. Would it be terrible of me to pursue it?" she asks, her voice filled with worry and anxiousness.

I contemplate her question for only a moment. "If he makes you happy then you do you, girl. What has Kira said?" I wonder.

"I asked her about it and she said and I quote 'Slay, Queen, Slay.' Which I'm taking as good." She laughs quietly.

Kira is the most typical teenage girl you will ever meet. The most tiktok and horse obsessed, new slang that no one understands teenager. If she's been around him and is OK with it then maybe he isn't such a bad guy after all.

"You know what, if you and Kira are happy and he's not as bad as everyone thinks then screw him sideways for all I care. You deserve some bloody happiness, girl," I encourage her.

"Oh, he's opening the door! Bye!" she squeals, and then she's gone.

Crows finally lets go of his pent up laughter before bending over, holding his stomach and wheezing.

"She calls him Eggy?!" His whole body practically vibrates with laughter, which ignites my own. It's contagious. I definitely need to re-meet Eggy.

Twenty

〜

"I guess I'm starting?" I ask as we sit around the coffee table together.

"We can't keep going like this, at each others throats, and the only one that can stop that is you, so yes, please." Victor's formality seems to have reached a new high and though I can't blame him given the recent days antics, that doesn't change the fact that I wish he didn't feel he had to be anything but himself with me.

"You're right," I say with a deep breath, knowing what needs to come next. "I'm not trying to lead you both on. I've been honest, *so* honest with both of you because I do care, more than I'd like to admit, but I can't choose one of you and lose the other. I know how selfish that sounds, but it's true. I feel like I've lost so many people and I can't stand the thought of not having either of you in my life," I tell them both, my eyes focused on the fidgeting hands on my lap, unable to look at either of them, knowing how awful my words sound.

"I don't know about you, mate, but Char knows how I feel. She knows I love her and I fucking want her. Every fucking part of her and if that's not what you want, if this is just some fling, some fucking joke, then you need to tell her because I want a life with her." Crow's words tear at the strings that tether themselves to my heart, pulling on every wish I'd ever had of wanting someone to want and love me that way.

I smile weakly at Crow, both in gratitude and awe, before turning to a tight-lipped Victor. He doesn't say anything for a moment, nearly a moment too long as I begin trying to decipher what he's thinking through his facial expressions. A mission that is practically impossible with the blank expression on his face.

"I'm not sure why you would assume my feelings for her are a joke. I know I don't know her as well as you might but that doesn't change the fact that I've been able to be more open with her than I have with anyone in my life. I've never loved anyone in a romantic way, and if I'm being totally frank with you, the idea of loving her is killing me because it puts her in danger, but I do. I knew it from the moment she first came into my home and I realised that I didn't want her to leave." The words coming out of his mouth may have been about me but until now they've been aimed at Crow, but now he looks at me. His eyes shine beneath the dim living room lighting, "I don't care if I have to share you, I don't give a damn about you loving him as long as I get to love you too. As long as I get to love you, I have everything."

The revelation stuns me because although I had thought it through so many times and I knew I didn't want to lose one of them, I didn't ever contemplate having them both. I didn't let myself think that it was ever a possibility.

"I can't do that. I can't choose, but I don't want you, either of you to feel like you're not my first choice. I want both of you to be with someone that can give you everything, and I just don't know that I can do that, not only because of everything that is going on right now but also because I don't know for sure that I'll ever be able to choose and I don't want you to wait and miss out on someone else, on finding someone that can choose *just* you while you're waiting for me."

Crow and Victor don't look at me. They're looking at each other, their gazes intense, though they don't look hurt or angry, they look as though they're somehow communicating something without my knowledge. If I ever believed in telepathy, it would be in this moment. It seemed like they were having a conversation between themselves without any words being spoken.

"What if we don't want that? What if we both want you? Together? Do we get a choice in this?" Victor turns to look at me, slowly, ever so slowly as he speaks, his eyes trained on mine as my head spins between his and Crow's unrelenting gazes.

"Together?" I ask anyone that will answer, somewhat dumbfounded at the mere idea of them both taking me, having me.

"Why don't we show you?" Crow suggests as he lifts himself up from the armchair to kneel in front of me.

With Crow on his knees beneath me and Victor to my side, I feel undeniably nervous. Not the bad kind of nervous, but the kind of nervous that makes me want to nod my head and tell them yes. Yes to whatever you want, anything you'll offer, *always* yes. Victor edges closer, his thigh tight against mine as he looks at Crow and nods, before gently moving a few strands of my hair away from my neck, behind my shoulder. Everything seems to be going in slow motion as he gives me time to say no, to stop whatever is about to happen. I can't fathom what *is* about to happen and yet not a single part of me wants to stop it.

Crow's rough hands run along the top of my thighs, making me thankful that I wore shorts, allowing him to touch every part of me that he wishes too. I find myself watching him intently as his hands begin pulling my legs apart, running his hands along the inside of my thighs, higher and higher, until he's so close. So close to my core, doing so little and yet doing so much at the same time, making me feel like every atom, every inch of me is ablaze with want and need.

Victor chooses that exact moment to begin coating kisses along my neck, and despite my need to not seem so desperate for them, my body takes control over my mind, my senses. My body arches, my core towards Crow and my neck perfectly placed for Victor in a desperate attempt to beg them, to plead with them - hoping that they never stop.

"That's it, pretty girl, let us in," Victor whispers in my ear, only magnifying the tension I feel, knowing that this is real, knowing that they're both here, giving me more than I ever anticipated wanting, let alone having. I try to catch my breath as they devour me, even knowing that being anything but breathless around them is impossible.

Crow's fingers move tantalisingly slowly as he grazes along the material of my shorts, pushing them aside, as well as the underwear beneath them, leaving his fingers stroking me gently. I like to think that I'm not completely inexperienced and innocent but in this moment, I feel like I've never been touched before and wonder why I've never initiated this very touch sooner. Victor's hands begin kneading at my breasts as he continues to place his lips along my collarbone. He places kisses along my jaw and then my chest until he uses his teeth to pull down my vest, revealing my bare breasts. At any other moment, any other time in my life, I would be disgustingly embarrassed and shy being laid bare so freely before these men and yet in this moment, I feel so much desire for them that I can hardly stop myself from asking them, begging them to do more, to give me everything.

Before I have time to think about what is happening, Crow is pulling my shorts and underwear from beneath me, lifting me so easily to do so. He discards the useless material before lowering his head to my clit, leaving open mouthed kisses along my most sensitive area. Without thought, my hand finds his head, holding him in place, refusing to let go of this euphoric feeling.

"Fucking perfect, so tight," Crow mumbles as he licks and fills me, entering me for the first time with his fingers, forcing my body to arch further, push his head down even more. I've never needed someone, let alone two someones, so much in my life.

Victor sucks and bites lightly at my nipples, leaving me achingly close to the release I know they'll bring me. The touch from them both feels like it's reaching every soluble part of my body. I've never felt more alight and needy as what I do now.

"Please don't stop." I gasp, unwillingly letting out a moan of pleasure I had attempted to keep in from the moment they began touching me.

"Which one of us don't you want to stop, pretty girl?" Victor whispers with a sexy chuckle before putting his mouth back on one nipple, while kneading the other breast with his free hand.

"Both," I practically cry out, feeling my body pound back into them both as we seem to move as one. "Both of you", I moan, "don't stop, please." I beg, incapable of saying anymore as my head rears back and my body tenses, knowing how close I am to finishing all over Crow's hand.

Crows tongue joins his fingers at my entrance, using his other hand to rub his finger against my clit while Victor continues biting and sucking at my nipples, using his free hand to reach for the back of my head, pulling at my hair from the roots. The tingling pain only accentuates the pleasure coursing through me from their joined attentive touch.

"You gonna cum for us, baby girl? I wanna taste every fucking bit of how much you need us," Crow breathes out before returning his attention, his lips, his tongue and face back to penetrate every wall I had ever put up.

"Don't be greedy, I want to taste her pussy too," Victor says with a glance up at me as he gets on his knees beside Crow.

The mere sight of them both on their knees before me has me as close to orgasm as their touch. These men, so mighty and deadly in their appearance giving me everything, all of them just as I open myself up to them completely.

"Open wide for us pretty girl, let us in," Victor encourages as they nudge my thighs even further apart. The slight burn my body emits from being in a position I haven't before is diminished by the immense pleasure that takes its place as they simultaneously suck and lick, nibble and finger my entrance and my clit. Their hands alternate so that one of them continuously has their hands on my breasts, roaming along my nearly bare stomach, having only my vest left scrunched around my waist, leaving me completely bare beside it.

"You're close aren't you, baby? I can feel it." Crow practically roars out at the very moment that an unrecognisable sound comes from my lips. I don't even know whose hand, whose fingers it is, but the penetrative pleasure and the constant attention on my clit has my whole body seizing up as I reach orgasm and feel them licking every morsel from my core.

It's now as I come down from the high, watching them raising their heads from the one part of my body that has never been touched by anyone beside myself that I feel so unbelievably cold and shy, unable and unwilling to look either of them in the eyes.

"Don't go shy on me now, baby girl, you were lapping it up just a minute ago." Crow laughs huskily as he rises from his knees before reaching his arms around me and lifting me up in a cradle of sorts.

"No, seriously, put me down," I tell him assertively as I attempt to wiggle away from him.

"Take her into the bathroom," Victor tells Crow as he follows behind us, ignoring my pleas.

Crow doesn't say a word but does as Victor ordered, leading me to the bathroom. Victor puts a towel on the toilet seat and encourages Crow to sit me down which he does. I want to scream and run away. I know what's about to happen and no matter how much I am reeling from what just happened, having them see me so bare now that the moment has passed leaves me feeling more vulnerable than ever; and yet I know arguing to get away is pointless because they won't let me and the same part of me that enjoyed them devouring doesn't want them to let me go.

Victor turns on the water in the shower and puts soap and shower gel in the holder before coming to kneel before me once more.

His eyes penetrate mine, his gaze intense. He doesn't say a word as he lifts my vest top off me and discards it to one side. I subconsciously wrap my arms around my stomach, feeling more exposed than I ever thought possible in the harsh luminescent shining down on me. On every wobbly, nowhere near perfect part of me.

"We want you and until the moment you push us away and tell us no, we're going to have you. Do you understand me?" he asks. Though the words sound demanding and somewhat bossy, they fill my heart to pure explosion as I nod solemnly at him.

"Now that that's cleared up, let's get you in the shower," Crow says as he lifts me up once more and places me gently into an upright position so that I'm stood in the shower.

"This is awkward, I can definitely do this part alone," I whisper uneasily as Victor and Crow pick up a sponge each and begin leisurely covering my body in a soapy massage.

"Yeah, maybe you can, but it doesn't mean that you're going to," Crow tells me simply as he and Victor continue their assault on my senses.

I can feel the heat beneath my skin warming once more at their touch.

The confidence I had only moments ago comes back, the questions and worry in the back of my mind disappearing, waiting to resurface another time.

I want them, both of them and seeing their clothes become drenched, their bodies wet and obviously apparent through their clothes only makes me want them more.

I reach my hands forwards, one on each of their chests, their heads rising simultaneously as they wonder where my touch may lead.

"What are you doing, pretty girl?" Victor asks huskily, his voice unsteady and unsure.

"Treating you the same way you treated me," I tell them quietly as I step out of the shower, turn it off, and lead them both into the bedroom, feeling the cold hit my every nerve, only inciting the excitement and confidence in me once more.

"You don't have to do this, babe, we didn't do it so that we'd get something back," Crow tells me.

I take my time, taking off both of their tops and trousers, leaving them only in their boxers.

I push them both gently onto the bed so that they're lay down next to one another, face up, eyes intent, watching me and my every move. Their eyes are both so dark and filled with desire and a hungry passion that I can't wait to set free.

"I know, but I want to. I want both of you," I tell Crow as I crawl onto the bed between them both. "I want you both *so* badly," I whisper into his ear, watching as his Adam's apple sways.

I haven't done anything like this before and yet when knelt above them, I feel like the most in control, surreal goddess. I feel like I could do or say anything and they'd let me.

I begin to drizzle soft kisses along their chests, taking it in turns, to be sure I give them both my complete attention, or as much of it as I can between them.

I take a deep breath, reeling in the courage I know I need for the next part of my not very well thought out plan.

I pull down Victor's shorts, taking his cock in my hand before using my other hand to pull down Crow's boxers and placing my lips over his cock.

Crow sucks in a shocked gasp while Victor lets out a soft moan. *This* makes me feel like a god. And I love it.

I bring my tongue around Crow's manhood, bobbing my head up and down while doing the same with my hand to

Victor's hard shaft. Crow's hand reaches my hair, his fingers tangling within it, pulling and pushing my head exactly where he wants it. I take in as much of him as I can before gagging.

"Shit, I'm so-"

I look up at Crow, his eyes filled with worry.

"Don't stop, I like it," I tell him, feeling the streaks rolling down my cheeks. His eyes fill with dark curiosity as he looks at me knowingly and pushes my head back down onto his dick.

"Fuck, I need some of that before I cum," Victor ushers out, his eyes dazed and filled with craze as he watches me take Crow in my mouth. My hand doesn't stop moving on his cock, the continuous rocking motion becoming more natural to me.

I take my mouth from Crow's cock, taking it in turns between them both. My head bobs from one of their cock to the other, a motion, accompanied by their hands on my body that makes me want to scream with the tension and passion filling me.

"I want you. I really, really need you to fill me. Please," I beg, feeling my body arch without my telling it too. My pussy is wet, drenched at the sight of them both being so turned on.

Crow lifts himself up from the bed, pulling his boxers off completely before settling behind my bent over body.

"Keep sucking his dick for me, baby. Don't stop," he tells me. I nod and continue, hearing Victor's moans and grunts of pleasure as he grips my hair and forces my head down over and over again. My core is desperate, my body shaking.

Crow's fingers take place inside of me, the need to be filled finally coming close to being granted.

"Can I take you, baby?" Crow asks as his cock grazes my entrance in place of his fingers.

"As long as Victor will after. I want you both," I tell him, my mouth coming back down to Victor's cock, moaning and arching my body in an attempt to rectify the fire filling me.

"Tell me if it hurts too much," Crow pants out as his cock begins gently filling me. My body takes a moment to accommodate to his size. It feels like my insides are vibrating to adjust to fit him inside of me. The fire felt like it was being quenched by pain for mere seconds before it comes roaring back.

"Fuck, I can't do this for long. You're so fucking tight, baby. I'm gonna cum any second," Crow all but growls at me before steadily pumping his thick shaft into me, causing my head to move and bob even further on Victor's drenched dick.

"You're fucking beautiful, look at you," Victor whispers out as he watches me. My speed picks up, my tongue rallying around the end of his cock each time I come up for air. Each time I gag when he pushes my head so far into him, my eyes tear up and the pain and submission I feel so willing and desperate to give them turns me on as much as the actions taking place.

Crow's body and cock pounding into me send me into a frenzied woman, my hands roaming over Victor's body, desperate for more.

Victor lifts me so that Crow is holding me up by my legs, not taking a single second to do anything but pushing his cock unto me harder and faster while Victor takes the opportunity to rub his cock along my clit, making me cry out with pleasure, unable to contain myself with the onslaught of touch being handed to me.

"Please, please," I cry, tears streaming down my face.

"Please what, baby girl?" Crow grinds out, his voice taking on a dangerously dark tone.

"Please don't stop," I beg, matching his every move with my own as my pussy desperately seeks out every inch of his cock.

Victor's teeth are latched onto my neck, bringing the painful passion back to light. The pain fires up and ignites my need for them. My mouth lets out the most sensual cries of pleasure I've ever heard before I feel one final pulse from Crows cock as he roars into my ear before he pulls it out and spins me around, telling Victor to finish me off.

Victor wastes no time, filling me once more with his giant manhood. I cry out as he does, craving more of his lips as he

165

places them along my neck while Crow does the same on the other side, my head resting back against Victor.

Crow plays with my clit while Victor grunts and fills me repeatedly in a motion that pushes my nipples into Crows chest. Victor pulls my hair so that my head is next to his before snatching my lips in a criminally chaotic kiss.

"I'm about to cum in you, pretty girl," Victor tells me.

"OK." I squeal out, reaching my own orgasm just as I feel the final pumps from his cock as he empties his load into me, mixing with Crow's.

"You're ours, well and fucking truly ours now," Crow whispers as they carry my drained and limp body to the bed. They take a side each, our heavy breathing mixed together as I cuddle into them both, feeling their orgasms leak out of me.

"Our girl, you got that, beautiful?" Victor asks. I nod my head, my eyes already closed as I mumble a yes and feel myself drifting off to sleep.

Twenty-One

I don't tell Victor and Crow that Liam has texted me. It is two am when I wake up to get a glass of water, nestled between the two of them, that I manage to sneak out into the kitchen without waking them and it is at that moment when I check my phone and find the message that confounds me.

Liam - Call me and I'll tell you everything.

He's been calling me since I got here the other evening, and I have yet to answer any of his calls or texts. I don't need proof to believe what Gray and Crow had told me. I believe them both wholeheartedly, but this text has my mind reeling.

I make sure I am far enough away from the closed bedroom door before calling him. I don't want Crow or Victor to overhear. They'll likely snatch my phone off me and insist I don't contact him again. Understandably so, given the situation and the recent revelations about him.

He answers on the first ring.

"How's my little girl doing?" I'm not sure what has happened in the last few days, but his voice sounds even more creepy now than it ever has before. Maybe it is just because I have been made aware of what he is really like.

"Don't call me that. What is it you need to tell me?"

"Oh, tut tut, don't you want to talk pleasantries first?" he asks. I can practically hear the snide smile on his face.

"Just tell me whatever it is. I haven't got time for this," I tell him nervously.

"Where was Crow when he left you?" he asks mischievously.

"Have you been watching us?" If I didn't believe Crow and Gray before, I certainly do now.

"I have eyes and ears everywhere. Where was he?" he asks again.

"With Dad. So we're not even pretending you're the good guy now?" I ask hesitantly. He doesn't seem to be attempting to cover the evil emitting from himself.

"You didn't answer my calls or texts. It's not hard to figure out why. Someone told you."

"So it's true? You were in on it?" I ask, knowing that he knows what I mean. The kidnapping.

"Yes, and I'd do it again in an instant. Now back to Crow, what was he doing with your dad?"

"Why? What's the point of this?" I ask curtly, not wanting to waste anymore time than needed on his line of questioning.

"He may have done some research into me, at least I'm assuming it's him that figured it out, but I've got my own information about him. He's an O'Banian. I suspect he's one of the sons." I recognise the name but have no idea why or where from.

"What's an O'Banian?" I ask, hating that I don't already know.

"I thought you'd be all caught up on this. The O'Banians are the Irish Mafia. They dabble within the police and the FBI. They're more tainted and potent than the rest of us put together. They send informants, undercovers to whoever they're interested at taking over or merging with. I have proof that he's one of them." I don't know what to say. He can't be right. That is ridiculous. Crow has told me about his family, his brothers. He wouldn't hide something like that from me. I am sure of it, and yet the niggling suspicion in the back of my mind doubts my own certainty.

"You're lying," I quip.

"Pay attention, little girl. He is an O'Banian. Plain and simple. Take of that what you will, but don't assume I'm the only liar around here."

"Are you the one that put the mark on me?" I ask, changing the subject. I'm not sure about Crow being an O'Banian, but I do know he is keeping things from me, that much is for sure.

I trust him endlessly. I trust him with my life, but that doesn't mean that I trust him not to lie or keep things from me. I know there is more to him, something he is hiding. That's when the reminder of the number on my phone and code words entered my mind. They aren't the Cobras, whoever he is talking to, but who is it? I need to find out.

Liam sighs, seemingly unsure of how to answer my question.

"I didn't, but I suspect I know who did. Be careful, girl. I might be a bad guy, but there are worse than me in the world. I would have looked after you well if I'd had you as a girl." The pleasure I can hear in his voice makes me want to be sick. He would have looked after me? I dread to think what that even means.

"Goodbye, Liam." I hang up, reeling from the conversation.

I immediately find the contact that Crow had added and informed me to ring if I needed them. My finger hovers over the name, wondering what would happen if I did call them.

Kenny. Down Viper Spring. I remind myself.

I press the call button and wait.

Two rings before it's answered by a man's breathy low tone.

"Tell me the code and what the problem is," he tells me. My stomach flips anxiously.

"Down Viper Spring. It's Charlie," I tell the stranger.

"I know who it is. What's wrong?" he asks.

"Who are you?" I ask lamely, knowing that this isn't how it works.

There's silence at the end of the line.

"You're only to call if it's an emergency."

"Please, I need to know," I beg.

"My name is Kenny. Ask Crow. Only call if it's an emergency, Charlie, this is a busy line. Oh and I won't tell anyone just yet about your little chat with Liam, or this one." The man chuckles.

The line disconnects at the same moment I throw my phone down and look around the room, wondering if there are hidden cameras. That can't be right though. This is Victor's home. Despite the fact that he hadn't ever told me so, I had no doubt that it was protected both physically and through any forms of hijacked technology. It has to be. All members, specifically those in the inner circle, are protected ferociously.

I pick my phone up again before realising that it must be the phone that's been hacked. It has to be. Whoever *Kenny* is, why is he willing to cover for me? It makes no sense.

The last ten minutes has left me with more questions than answers. I rub a hand over my eyes, the exhaustion of the last few weeks finally hitting me. My whole body feels completely drained. I take a seat on the sofa, knowing that one way or another, I need to find some answers to the various questions I have. Who put the mark on me and how the hell do I make it go away? What is Liam's endgame in all of this? What is Crow lying about? Where is Gray? And finally, what on earth am I supposed to do with the two of them? Can I really be with them both? Is it possible or will it end with all of us heartbroken?

I take to Google on my phone, uncaring any longer about whether or not my phone has been hacked, if *Kenny* can cover for the phone calls, he can cover for this too. Or not. I don't care anymore.

I search up the O'Banians. There are so many news articles

but every single one I click on seems to have so little information on. And then the articles start disappearing. I mean, literally disappearing. I click on each article and then my phone turns off. I turn it back on, search it up again, and the article will be gone. I do the same thing four times before realising that it is *him*. It has to be. That's how he knew about the phone call with Liam and it's how he's doing this. It has to be. Does that mean Crow really does have something to do with the O'Banians, or is there another reason why Kenny or whoever else is attempting to stop me finding out more? Is there another reason? Maybe these O'Banian dudes are just really bad news, but that didn't seem like enough of a reason. Or is he just toying with me?

I press the call button again, this time ready to give this Kenny guy a mouthful rather than a nervous few questions.

"I told you to call if there was an emergency. I'm not an agony aunt, Charlie," the mystery voice says down the phone. I can hear the amusement in his voice.

"Why are you playing with me? Who are the O'Banians? And what gives you the right to decide what I do and don't get to see on *my* phone?" I whisper-scream at him, feeling my heart rate rise with frustration.

"Women are so dramatic. Maybe I'm doing it for your own good. Go and wake Crow up and ask him. I'm a gossip, but I'm not allowed to be right now, so sadly I can't tell you anything. Nighty night, nosy."

"You're a dick," I seethe before hanging up again, hearing his cackle-like laugh before I do.

Maybe I shouldn't have called him a dick. I might actually need him at some point. Well, shit.

Twenty-Two

"If it's happening, I'm going," I insist as I rummage around Victor's bookshelf looking for the book I was reading last night. I swear he's hidden it from me. Well, probably not, but I have no other solution as to where it's gone so I'm blaming him.

"You can't. Do you have any fucking idea how dangerous it is for you, Char?" Crow remarks, throwing his hands up in the air in frustration.

"He's right. It's not safe. I'm sure we can think up a way for you to have fun here," Victor tells me, flirting between the line of being serious and sexy as he takes a step towards me and places his hands on my hips.

I dip away from him, knowing that if I let either one of them touch me that I'll cave.

"No. You'll both be there! How much more protected can I be?" I ask them, knowing it's a low blow but also well aware that they'll take it as a hit to their ego if they have to say they can't protect me.

"Charlie, if me and Mr Kiss My Girl agrees, you know I have to be right." It's back to Crow. They're tag teaming me. Against me.

"Mr Kiss *Our* Girl," Victor corrects him.

The simple correction gives me flutters, sending me into a girly dizzy spell that fills me with the same love and adoration that they've both centred around me since the declaration of care. Well.

"Will you stop and listen to us for a minute, Charlie?" Victor says as he stops me in my tracks and backs me up against Crow. I'm in a sandwich. I'm the filling. My mind takes even that thought into a dirty frenzy, but I stop myself before I start something I know will end with me vulnerable and agreeable.

"You can touch me up all you like but I'm still going," I tell them.

No one thought the party would still be going on tonight but since it is, I want to go. I get that it could be dangerous, though with the heightened security, I imagine everything will be fine. After last week's attack, I hardly imagine they'll be scrimping by on protecting the Club.

"I just want one night to be a teenager. Everything is so chaotic right now, I just need one night. That's it. I've never even been to a real party. Please," I turn as I finish, hating that I'm begging them. I know they're worried, and I get why they are, but that doesn't change my motivation to go.

They eye one another steadily before Victor relents and nods at Crow.

"Fine, but you do not leave our side, do you understand?" Crow asks. I hardly let him finish before I'm nodding enthusiastically at them both and running off to find my book again. I need to read. Then I can get ready.

"Not once, I swear." I smile as they simultaneously shake their heads in defeat.

The book is under the cushion. That's weird. I pick it up before skipping into Victor's bedroom to pick something to wear. I had asked Crow to go and get my clothes earlier this morning. It wasn't hard to tell that he didn't know what to

173

bring so literally grabbed a few handfuls out of each of my drawers and hoped for the best.

It's now that I'm away from them that I wonder why I haven't mentioned the phone call with Liam.

I was going to. Before falling asleep again last night, I had told myself that I would ask them both about it. Even though the conversation with Liam centred around Crow, I am sure Victor knows more than he is telling me too.

I'm not sure what stopped me. Or rather, I perhaps didn't want to admit that I was worried about how they would react, worried that they would cover up my concerns or be frustrated with me for not telling them sooner.

Dad still insisted I go to the doctor this morning, which I had completely forgotten about until he rang me twenty minutes before I was supposed to be there, reminding me of it. I'm not sure why he is so insistent on the check ups when nothing is wrong. It is long, boring, and to add to matters, I am met with a grumpy doctor that is not our normal doctor. He isn't rude, he is just very reserved and seems unwilling to interact, which is always fun.

I'm not sure that he does it on purpose, chances are he is just busy and sick of people. I can't say I blame him if that is the case. I would be bored stiff of seeing people day in and day out too if I were in that situation. Dad used to get everyone check ups with the Club Doctor every few months but he hasn't done it in a few years. I wonder what made him change his mind so suddenly.

I have spent the afternoon jazzing myself up in Victor's bedroom, insisting that he and Crow leave me alone to have some girl time. I have spent the time pampering every inch of skin I have. Shaving, waxing, moisturising, creaming, and preening. My body feels completely brand new. Sleek, slim, and when

I look in the mirror before leaving, I am more impressed than I ever thought I would be when I was planning out my clothes this morning. It isn't often I look at myself and think I look nice, but I know that what I am wearing will blow Victor and Crow away. And as much as I hate the idea of dressing up for a man, or two men in this case, imagining their faces seeing me in this only makes me want to wear it even more.

Just the thought of the acts that had taken place in the recent days with them sends shivers down my spine, a fire filling the frenzied and constant need I seem to have when around or thinking about them.

I had crimped my hair, loving the volume it gives it as well as the slim shape it gives my face.

I put on some blood red lipstick, black mascara, and some smoky eyeshadow.

I didn't bother with foundation, blusher, or contour. I never usually wear makeup, so having on what I already do makes my face feel full as it is. Plus I'm not great at doing it in the first place, so I am sticking with the safe, easy options.

I love makeup on other girls. They always make it look incredible and flawless, but applying makeup is not a skill I have and most of the times I've tried it, I look orange. Not the look I'm ever after and yet the only one I seem to be able to get right, so it's easier to just avoid it all together.

I had decided on red strappy heels, a black skin tight dress that showed just enough cleavage, accentuated my curves, and is short enough to make my legs look longer than they really are.

I had chucked a leather jacket on top, mainly just because it is cold and I need some sort of cover or I'll never make it to the club, let alone inside to enjoy myself, but also because it is my favourite one that I wear with just about everything.

Dad picks me up and drops me off outside the club, the boys saying they'd meet me there. They didn't mind me being away from them since I was with my dad.

The music at the club is monstrously loud. I am only at the

gates and can hear it already. I am surprised it is still going on but as Crow had said, we can't live our lives avoiding the very things that we want for the fear of something bad happening. He is right.

There are at least a hundred people stood outside, smoking and drinking, swaying from side to side, probably so intoxicated that they are completely unaware of what is going on around them.

I have never been drunk like that, and I never want to be either. I hate the idea of being in a state, physically and mentally, where I'm not fully in control of what I am doing or saying. I mean, I got that it could be fun, that it was a release that everyone needs at some point. I just never want to be in a position where I have no control. That's my worst nightmare come to life.

My goal is to find Crow, Victor, and Alice (and maybe even Eggy) and just be a teenager for a little while. A few drinks won't hurt.

"Yo, Char!" I'm nearly at the door and turn towards the voice that I instantly recognise as Crow's. He is walking straight towards me, having spotted me before I saw him.

He pulls me inside of the club, and I find myself immediately surrounded. It's packed in here. How anyone is dancing is beyond me. There's hardly space to move or breathe, let alone actively dance to whatever the hell is echoing over the speakers.

Crow hands me a drink. I take a sip and recoil in shock.

"Fucking hell, Crow!" I exclaim. "What are you trying to do to me?" I ask with a laugh.

Vodka, and vodka alone, is filling the red plastic cup he has handed me. It burns my throat and starts a fire in my chest from breathing through the cold air outside.

A cup later and a chat with a still working, but ignoring any customer that isn't me Alice, and I can feel the alcohol taking effect on me.

I don't recognise most of the people here. A few say hello,

bump into me by accident, and apologise, or try to flirt, but I push most away or simply ignore them.

I'm sat on a bar stool talking to Alice about a man in the corner that looks like he's about to be sick. His friends are around him trying to get him in the taxi outside to get him home, and Alice is informing me that this far too drunk man is a regular that does this every time a drop of anything alcoholic passes his lips.

Crow went to the bathroom about twenty minutes ago and hasn't yet come back. I wonder what he's doing. I wonder where Victor is too, I've not seen him anywhere.

I tell Alice I'll be back soon, down another cup of vodka that I know I'll soon regret, and unsteadily clamber off the bar stool in search of Crow and Victor.

So much for not letting me leave their sides. I can't even find them, let alone stay with them.

Through the main hall, I enter the corridors, leading me to the quietest part of the club. The people in the party were only allowed in the main hall or to the toilets to the left of the main hall. Crow wouldn't have used them though. A lot of the men have designated rooms here, and chances are he would have gone to his, so that's where I start.

Before I get very far though, in one of the guest rooms, I hear roars of laughter, male laughter, and decide to check inside to see if Crow has found some of his friends that he's got distracted with.

I can feel my body moving from side to side without my consent. My head seems to be swimming in thoughts that I can't straighten or comprehend.

I crash into the wall through my drunken stupor, but quickly lift myself from it in the fear of someone realising how drunk I am.

I'm still in control. My body is just a little out of sync with my mind. That's all.

I push open the door, apparently forgetting formalities and

knocking in my drunken state and find two guys that I vaguely recognise.

I can't pinpoint their names. Sober me would probably know, but vodka drinking Charlie has absolutely no idea.

I think the one on my right, the one dancing on the bed, might be Matt. Or is it Max? It might even be Marty. It starts with an M, that much I'm sure of. I think. He's got ice blonde hair and the darkest eyes. He's always covered in cuts and bruises from fighting. My dad doesn't like him but has never had enough evidence of bad behaviour to get rid of him.

The one on the left looks similar with light hair. This one has darker streaks through his though, a disgusting smirk stuck on his face, and clothes that reek of weed.

Stoner and maybe Matt. Wait no, we'll call him Marty.

I notice probably a moment too late that there's coke laid out on the dressing table in the middle. This must be one of their rooms. There are pictures and posters all over the place, men's clothing and odd shoes hanging here, there and everywhere.

"Sorry, wrong room." I salute to them for whatever stupid reason as I go to leave but I am pulled back by hands on my waist.

How did they get that close to me without me realising?

"Get off me!" I scream, but watch as I struggle in the ones embrace, the other shuts and locks the door.

Oh fuck.

Why did I drink?

I can feel it. My arms, my legs, my whole body. It's not as capable. Not as strong or decisive as what I am in a fight when sober.

He lets me go but I don't move.

It's Matt/Marty that locked the door. He's blocking the door. Stoner is watching me with a smug expression plastered on his face.

"You think you're so high and mighty being his daughter, don't you?" Matt asks me as he inches closer.

"Oh shut up and let me out." I don't let my fear show or at least I don't think I do.

I'm not stupid. I know what stupid guys like these think they can get but they're not getting it from me.

Before I have chance to turn to see Stoner laughing, I feel the heaviest sensation against the side of my head and collapse to the floor from it, my eyes becoming dark, the room dim as I feel nothing but heavy darkness.

I wake in a new room, my eyes adjusting just enough to see that I'm not in any place that I recognise. How did they get me out of the Club and somewhere new without me waking? I must be in the club. My mind must just be playing tricks on me.

Is this about the mark that had been placed on me? Or is it purely bad luck?

My eyesight is blurry, my head drumming. I can see their lips moving, but I can't hear them. I can see five, no six of them even though I know there's only two. The same two.

I try to move, to get up but Matt, or was it Marty? No, Matt is on me in an instant, pinning my arms down from behind me, above my head.

My body is shaking, and I can feel my cheeks are wet. I'm not sure if it's me crying, or blood from whatever Stoner guy hit me with. I can't tell.

I feel like my head's been flushed down the toilet ten times. Nothing I can see is making sense. I can't hear him but I can see Matt laughing. My legs are flailing, kicking. I'm screaming.

I can't understand what's happening.

I need to get them off me, but no matter how much I kick or try to move my arms and fling my body from side to side, nothing's happening.

Am I even moving?

Stoner guy says something to Matt and they both laugh.

Stoner guy punches me. It happens so quickly that I don't

even have time to move my head away to stop him. He hits me again, and all I can feel is the swelling and my head hitting the floor as he lifts it up with one hand and hits me with the other.

I can see the blood. I don't know how I can see it, but my eyes are red.

Everything looks red and bleary. He hits over and over and over again for what feels like hours.

I can hardly see now. My eyes must be swollen or blocked with blood.

He stamps on my stomach with his boots and my automatic reaction is to curl up to protect myself but with my arms being held down, all that happens is my legs moving, but I'm just giving him more of a chance to get his leg in just the right place to do it again.

I can hear myself screaming, I'm just not sure if its really happening, if I'm physically screaming or if it's just in my head that I'm rejecting this moment, in denial that this is happening.

No one in the club is supposed to hurt anyone, let alone women. It's not because I'm special but because I'm supposed to be able to look after myself.

They know that the music is too loud for anyone to hear me. They know no one is allowed into that part of the club unless they are a club member.

I don't know if they were going to do it anyway or if it was just a matter of wrong time, wrong place. They're at least smart enough to know that they won't get caught right now and that's what scares me the most. There's no one here to come and save me, and I seem incapable of saving myself.

They're talking, probably shouting, but I still can't hear.

They're laughing at me.

Matt is slapping my face. I can't feel it. It doesn't hurt. The only reason I know is because of my head lolling to each side as I watch the actions take place.

My head hitting the floor when they hit me and being thrown to either side when they slap me.

My whole body feels I've been run over by an arctic lorry. I don't think my body's ever felt so weak.

So scared.

I'm sure I'd normally be filled with rage in this situation, but all I want to do is cry, sob, scream and ask for someone, anyone to come and save me. To help me.

Stoner guy gets down between my legs. He lifts my tattered dress up, rips my underwear off me, and tosses it aside.

I use every last ounce of energy and strength I have to try and twist and turn every part of my body out of their grasp, but all that I get in turn is Matt hitting my face more. Stoner guy is brushing my lower half, and more screaming fills my mind.

Matt has worked out the obvious. That even without him holding onto me that I can't move. He's knelt on my arms now, just in case and pulls down the top of my black strapless dress.

His face goes down towards my breasts just as Stoner pulls apart my incapable stupid legs.

Matt is biting me. Biting me. And I can hardly feel it because all I can think about is what's about to happen and what the monster in front of him is going to do next.

Matt sits back, weight killing my arms, probably turning them in all kind of directions they're not supposed to be in.

He's pulling my hair, sneering in my face.

Forcing me to look at Stoner.

I do.

He's already got his trousers pulled down and his cock out.

It's disgusting.

I think I'm going to be sick.

I'm gagging, coughing, spluttering and retching.

I'm screaming, fighting, in pain, not capable of saving myself.

He's holding my legs apart no matter how much I try to fight it. My body is at the end of its tether.

He pushes himself inside of me and it hurts.

It hurts so much that I feel the screaming off my lips change from a scream to an outright cry. I sound like a little child desperate for her mother.

But I don't have anyone to come and save me.

He's pumping his body in and out of me as Matt slaps me some more.

It feels like a fire is going off inside of me. Stretching, scratching, and a burning fire is killing me. I feel like I'm being torn apart.

It hurts so badly I feel like I'm going to pass out.

Matt has a knife in his hand and I can hardly move to watch what he's doing.

My whole body is moving on the floor from the movements happening within me.

I'm crying. I'm begging. I'm asking a God I've never believed in, I'm asking anyone to stop this. To save me. To give me something to hold onto.

I feel a scratch on my neck, though when I look I know it must be so much more than that. There's a knife on my neck.

I feel no pain when he drags it up onto my face, across my cheek.

He stabs my arm and I feel a searing pain both inside of me from the monster inside of me but also from the knife that is being repeatedly stabbed into my body.

He puts it into my stomach.

Passes it to Stoner who takes a break and shoves it into my leg. Again. And again.

My stomach. Again.

They're going to kill me.

I'm going to die today.

My body isn't my own anymore. I feel like I'm watching it from above. From a whole different place.

And then the door opens.

My sight is blurry, my mind a puddle of despair and horror as I attempt to call for help from whoever the new entry into the room may be. I look up, my sight clearing slightly and I see two faces, both of which make my throat feel like it's being strangled. The air leaves my lungs, the room becomes smaller, my mind confused as I look upon the face I always assumed would forever be my saving grace.

It's Gray, but my brother hasn't come to save me. And neither has the man stood next to him.

Epilogue

D iary Entry #1

I will never sign my story again, for my body has been signed in ways that kill me, and I never wish to instill that horror onto anyone or anything, not even these sheets of paper beneath my hand, but for this one time, for once, for the only time there will ever be - I'm signing my story for you.

CK
    Charlie Keller

To be continued...

You can order Part 2
Signed For Him by J.R Dust

Afterword

Thank you so much for reading Signed For You! It is something so so close to my heart that I've even working on for such a long time now. I truly appreciate every single person that takes the chance to read it.

If you enjoyed it, please consider leaving a review. Reviews are so important to us authors!

If you're interested in finding out about future releases, talking about this story and any future releases of mine and just generally chatting with other like minded book lovers, you can join my Facebook group here -

J.R Dust's Book Besties

Acknowledgments

I have so many people that I want and need to thank for helping me finally getting the first of many ideas published!

Thank you to my amazing editor for making this book what it is today - Magnolia Author Services (she is an absolute star and puts up with A LOT from me. I am constantly harassing her with questions and new ideas!)

Thank you to my wonderful PA for helping me organise everything and anything I've thrown your way!

A HUGE thank you to my Beta and ARC readers for the crazy amount of support and love you have shown for this story and the upcoming releases. I could not have made this story what it is without your input, thoughts, brutal honesty and care.

A massive appreciation message to the lovely - Forgetyounotdesigns (find her on instagram) for making my teasers and the beautiful cover! She is the sweetest and so so helpful!

A HUGE shout out to my incredible ARC and Beta readers who have been the most sensational support imaginable. You are the absolute dream team and I can not thank you all enough for being as sweet, kind and helpful as you have been.

And finally, to my babies (because they're the best - yes, I'm biased but they totally are), my partner (who is a major introvert but beyond supportive in his own way. He will never read this unless I shove it in his face - literally, but I love and appreciate him endlessly anyway), my mum (for being my first and biggest fan in life, writing, reading and everything else I've drove her crazy with) and my youngest sister (for talking to me non stop about my books, stories, helping me with playlists, tiktoks and just generally being a cool teenager 😎)

And to you, my readers for going on this ride with me! I will be forever grateful to everyone single person that has picked up this book and any future books I release.

Printed in Great Britain
by Amazon

23056305R00109